PLUM CREEK

A NOVEL

SEQUEL TO VENCIL

PLUS THREE BONUS SHORT STORIES

FRANK SHIMA

Dedicated to my wife, Robin, who helped me immensely with Plum Creek.

TABLE OF CONTENTS

PROLOGUE

It is, what it isn't.

What it is, isn't home.

What it isn't, is Plum Creek.

What it is, is trapped.

CHAPTER 1
NO PLACE LIKE HOME

Plum Creek because it begins there. But it doesn't end there. It might have ended there if not for the fire.

The farm in Plum Creek was no place like home. To call this a farm would probably make all other farms feel bad and want to be called something else. My mom called it a dump. I thought calling it a dump would make all dumps feel bad and want to be called something else.

The barn roof sagged in the middle and rested on the floor of the hayloft which meant that no hay could be stored inside. The sheds and the chicken coop were missing doors and windows. The house at least had those, maybe the ones from the sheds and the chicken coop. Not much more could be said for it. It hadn't been painted inside or out probably since it had been built. There wasn't a level floor in the house. Eventually, you got used to walking and sitting at an angle.

The best thing that I could say about this farm is that it wasn't ours. We were renting a farm on Plum Creek. Whatever work we did on the farm went toward the rent. According to my dad, our work didn't seem to be worth much because we never seemed to make a dent in what we had to pay each month.

My dad had been offered a job in the creamery, but he didn't think he'd like working inside all day. I didn't understand because he would work fewer hours a day than he did on the farm. He said farming was in his blood. I sure hoped it wasn't in mine. If it was, I'd have to figure a way to get it out.

To make things worse, for me anyway, is that this farm was across the road from our old farm on Plum Creek. Each day I had to avoid looking to the west so I wouldn't be reminded of what I was missing. I wanted to sneak onto our old farm and play in the pasture and woods, but I knew I would just feel worse when I had to leave.

This house did have electricity which meant we now had television. Uncle John said we were spoiled. He just couldn't see a use for television. I didn't understand why everything had to be useful.

Even I had to be useful. I still had to do farm chores three times a day. When we lived in town for a few months, I had only one chore, taking out the garbage. My friend, Pete, told me he didn't even have to do that. This made my farm chores seem even harder.

One of my chores was to burn the trash. I had either let it go for too long or the neighbors had decided to secretly dump all their trash on us. I took it out to the burn pile, wheelbarrow load after wheelbarrow load. There was a lot to burn. Instead of burning it little by little, I decided to burn the whole huge mound of trash all at once. I don't know if I had gotten lazy or I just wanted to see the towering flames reach above the trees.

This was when I started to think that I had made a mistake. There were two things I hadn't thought of. The unusually dry summer we were having and the unusually windy day. Burning papers and embers flew through the air. Flames started in another dry patch.

I ran back to the barn, grabbed a bucket, and filled it with water from the water trough. I hurried to the burn pile and tossed the water on the fire. It seemed to put out a little of the fire. After about a dozen trips, the flames had died down. I then sat on the ground, relieved and happy. For some reason, I had enjoyed it. Burning the trash had never been so much fun.

Then I saw a car belonging to our neighbor, Tupa, speeding and honking its way into our driveway. The car braked to a sliding stop next to our house. He and his three kids jumped out, each carrying a pitchfork.

"Your pasture's on fire! Your pasture's on fire!"

They ran through our farmyard toward our pasture. My dad and mom flew out of the barn following them. Three other cars turned into our driveway, the last belonging to Uncle John.

I stomped on burning grass until it felt like my shoes were burning up. Uncle John took off his coat and beat at the flames, turning the denim from blue to black. With all of our neighbors helping we managed to stop the advance of the fire. Then for some reason, the wind decided to reverse direction and fanned the flames on the other side toward the farmstead. We all ran around and stomped and fought but were unable to keep the fire from reaching the barn. Soon the barn was just a pile of ashes. We were so busy we hadn't noticed flames on the roof of the house. The fire department arrived and saved the house. Part of it anyway.

"The house is no longer livable," the fire chief told my mom.

"If you ask me, it wasn't livable before," she answered.

Totally exhausted, we sat by the cars. I looked back at the charred remains of the pasture. Half of it had been burned. The cows on the other side stood there eating grass as if nothing had happened.

I felt bad because I knew it had been my fault. Not only did I smell like smoke, but I also smelled like burned hair. My shoes had almost burned through as well. Then I started to feel the pain. I lifted my pantlegs and noticed huge, red blotches of skin. I jumped up and ran to the water trough. I pulled off my pants and stepped inside, water up to my waist.

I was thinking how good it felt when I looked over to see everyone pointing and laughing at me. They thought I was being funny. I guess I'd rather have them thinking that than have them blame me for starting the fire.

My mom ran from what was left of the house with a towel and the butter dish. She had me step out of the trough. That's when I noticed how bad the burns looked. She dabbed at my legs with the towel and slathered me with butter. I felt like our Thanksgiving turkey before my mom put it in the oven.

The laughter stopped when everyone got a look at my legs.

"Is it bad, Mom?"

"Not so bad, Jimmie. I've seen worse. It'll heal before you get married."

I couldn't imagine myself ever getting married so what she said didn't make me feel that much better.

"I wonder how that fire started," Tupa said.

"We were just doing a pasture burn and it got out of hand," my dad said, covering for me.

"It's a good thing the cows weren't caught in the fire, or we'd be having a barbeque now," Blaha said.

"Well, I got some beer if anyone wants one," my dad offered.

Nobody turned him down.

As my mom and I looked at the burnt-out house, she hugged me close.

"I noticed that fire long before anyone showed up. I wasn't going to say anything until it finished burning down that house. Now maybe we can finally move back to town."

CHAPTER 2

JIMMIE'S GANG

There are times I wonder why I did the things I do. This was one of them.

The air smelled different in town. I took in a deep breath. I inhaled the aroma of freshly cut grass. On the farm, there was the occasional smell of newly mowed alfalfa but most of the year, the air was filled with the odor from the barnyard and stink of manure in the pastures.

Yes, there was noise in town but even that was different. Instead of the roar of tractors and the sounds of cows, chickens, and horses, I heard the blare of car horns and the screech of tires on city streets.

As I walked toward downtown, I saw other kids playing and laughing and doing their best to ignore me. Why not? Most of them didn't know me. After four years, I was still the new kid in town.

When I reached Gambles Hardware, I knew I should have been home, but I had stayed out too late playing baseball. The sun had already set over the west end of Main Street. Streetlights had come on. I heard voices from the darkness in the alley next to the First National Bank. I stopped and listened.

"I can't fit in there! There's no way!"

"If you can't, I sure can't."

"This was your bright idea. You should have thought of this."

"I can't think of everything."

I took a few steps into the alley to see what was going on.

"Hey, you! Get lost," a voice yelled from the darkness.

"Who? Me?" I asked, instead of getting lost.

"Yeah, you!"

I turned to leave.

"No! Wait! Come back. You're small, aren't you?"

"Yeah, I guess."

"Then maybe you could help us."

"I guess."

"Quit guessing and get over here."

"I don't know. I should be getting home. It's late and…"

"I said get over here."

With small steps, I ventured into the darkness. That was a mistake. What was waiting there for me was worse than anything on the farm. Worse than getting kicked by a cow while crossing behind her when cleaning the gutters. Worse than stepping on a rusty nail when running through the yard. Worse than getting chased by our mean bull, Duke, nostrils flaring and sharp horns ready to show me who was boss.

"Don't take all night about it! Hurry up," the short one, Pickle, shouted. Even in dim light, I could see his snarl, yellow teeth, and the meanness in his eyes. I knew if I didn't do as he said, it would be better if Duke were waiting for me in the alley. The tall one, Bull, had a blank look on his face. He seemed resigned to his fate, like he would always do what Pickle wanted.

"What do you want?" I asked.

"We can't fit," Bull said.

"Can't fit? Where?"

"Through this window down here."

I looked at them and the window and figured they should have picked a bigger window.

"We need you to crawl through there for us."

"No. I don't think so. I'm not going in there."

"Yes. I think you are," Pickle said.

"I know you are," Bull said.

"It's dark in there. What do you want in there anyway?"

"None of your business," Pickle said.

"Yeah. None of your business," Bull echoed.

"You're right. It's none of my business. I'm going home."

"No. You're doing what we want."

"And what's that?"

"Nothing to it. You know how to open a door. Don't you?"

"Yes."

"Go through the window, go up the stairs, and then open the door here for us to get in."

"Why? What's in there anyway?"

"Just do it!"

I backed away but Bull grabbed me and started to stuff me through the window, head-first. The more I resisted, the more I didn't fit. The more I was hurting myself by scraping my arms and legs on the windowsill. Finally, I dropped down into darkness.

"What do you see?" asked Pickle.

"Nothing."

"What do you mean nothing."

"Like I said. Nothing. It's dark in here."

"Then turn on a light, why don't you?" Bull said.

"No. Don't be stupid. Here's a flashlight," Pickle said.

Instead of handing it to me, he tossed it down to me, hitting me on the head. It landed at my feet. I groped in the darkness. Finding it, I turned it on.

I pointed it into the darkness. At first, there wasn't anything interesting. Desks and chairs. A white lab coat like doctors wore. And then I saw something I had seen once before at my grandmother's funeral. A casket. And another. And another. The basement was filled with them.

Why did these two idiots want to break into a funeral home? I wasn't sure I wanted to know. But they were dying to get in.

I followed the light from the flashlight up the steps and to the side door. I turned the knob and opened it. Bull and Pickle charged toward me.

"You took your sweet time getting up here," Pickle said.

"You could have opened it yourself. If you had checked, you'd have seen it wasn't locked."

"Not locked? Why wouldn't they lock the door to the bank?"

"Maybe because…"

"Never mind. Let's get the money!"

They dashed past me. Bull knocked me to the floor, stomping on me on the way. I got up and tried to escape but Pickle grabbed me before I got out the door.

"Wait a minute," Pickle said. "You're not going anywhere."

"Let me out of here," Bull said. "Funeral homes give me the creeps."

"You picked the wrong building, Bull."

"Me? You said this was the bank."

"Never mind what I said. The bank is across the alley."

"Kid, come with us."

"I did what you said. Let me go home."

"No. We're not done with you yet."

They dragged me across the alley to another window that also was too small for them to crawl through. Unluckily for me, it wasn't too small for me to get through. Bull pried the window open with a crowbar. I expected alarms and bells to go off but there was only silence. Maybe it had one of those silent alarms I had heard about.

"Okay, you. Get in there. You know the drill."

Again, I resisted. Again, Bull shoved me through the window and dropped me on the floor into the darkness below. Again, Pickle dropped the flashlight on my head.

The basement was filled with row after row of filing cabinets, all taller than me. I wound my way through this maze until I found a stairway leading to the first floor. Trying not to make a sound, I tiptoed up the wooden stairs to the black and white tiled floor.

It was my first time in a bank. If I got caught, it would probably be my last. Rows of desks filled this area. A high counter topped by bars with openings marked for tellers stood against one wall. I didn't know what a teller was. They probably told people what to do with their money, I guess.

What would the police do if they found me in here? Shoot me?

"Hurry up in there, why don't you?" I heard Pickle shout from outside. "Open the door."

What was he trying to do? Get us caught? Except I would be the one who would be caught inside. Not them.

I followed the flashlight past a door with the lettering, MR. THOMAS MINAREK, BANK PRESIDENT. I then came to the front door with a sign that lied. It said, OPEN. When I tried to open the door, it was definitely *not* open.

"Hurry up!" Pickle shouted.

"Be quiet," I whispered. "Do you want us to get caught?"

"Open the door!" he shouted.

"I tried but it's locked."

"Well, unlock it!"

"I can't. You need a key. And I don't have one."

"Look around and find one, why don't you?"

"Okay," I whispered. But I knew I wouldn't find one. Why would you lock a door and leave a key inside? You took the key with you so you could get in the next day. I didn't try searching for a key and headed back toward the basement. Back to the basement window where Bull and Pickle could lift me out of the bank.

That's what I thought anyway. On the way down the steps, I heard a siren from off in the distance. It grew louder and stopped when it reached the bank.

"Let's get out of here!" Pickle shouted.

"Hey! What about me?" I shouted.

I heard footsteps running out of the alley.

"Hey, you two! Stop!" a policeman shouted.

"Ah, hell. Whoever they were, they're long gone now through that hole in the fence. We'll never find 'em."

But they would find me inside a bank.

"Here's the hole in the window. What were those two knuckleheads trying to do? Breaking into a funeral home?"

"Let's see what they were up to in there."

The good thing was they didn't know I was in the bank and that Bull and Pickle were trying to rob the bank. The bad thing was when they unlocked the door in the morning, they would discover me hiding in their basement.

CHAPTER 3

THE FREE MONEY CHECK

My whole world now consisted of darkness, pitch-black darkness. In the darkness, I pretended I was someplace else, someplace where I wasn't in trouble.

My only means of escape were my thoughts. I thought back to when I first moved to town.

The move from the farm to town brought many changes in my life. One element that didn't change was the kind of house in which we lived. While we did have electricity and television, we didn't have running water with indoor plumbing. A wood stove was still our only source of heat.

Our house in town had a dirt basement which usually held water that came up almost to the top step. This produced an interesting aroma as well as a breeding ground for rats.

Another thing that did not change was my mother's housekeeping. She had always preferred working outdoors and still didn't devote much time to chores inside the house. When she did sweep the floors, she had her own version of sweeping things under the rugs. Dirt, newspapers, and scraps of clothing were swept into the basement.

Shortly after we moved to town, my dad's stepfather moved in with us. This did not go over too well with my mother.

Most of the time, she couldn't tolerate my Grandpa Joe. The exception was when he got his pension check. I wasn't sure what a pension check was but since Grandpa Joe didn't work, it must have been free money. I even wondered why I didn't get this free money check.

On the days when he got the free money, she would be extra nice to him which meant being civil toward him. She would then be rewarded with some extra money to buy comic books or toys for me. Otherwise, she wouldn't be in the same room with him.

I'm afraid that I may partly have been the reason they didn't get along. It occurred on the farm when I was six years old. My folks had left me at home with my sixteen-year-old brother when they went to town to grind feed. My brother wandered off to Uncle John's place, leaving me home alone. I found myself on a stack of bales playing king of the castle. I then rearranged the bales to form tunnels inside with secret passageways.

Unfortunately, invaders found their way into the tunnels, and I was forced to take out my sword (the pocket knife my dad had given me) to ward off the enemy. That was how the twine on each bale was cut, converting a neat stack of hay bales into a heap of loosely strewn hay.

When my dad came home, I tried to explain about the invaders of the hay castle. For some reason, he didn't believe this was what had occurred. I knew he was going to scold me. That would be worse than if he took off his belt and led me to the woodshed. That was when I took off running. I dashed around the barn, with my dad in full pursuit.

My Grandpa Joe, who had come back with them, grabbed a pitchfork and ran after my dad as we rounded the barn for the first time. My mother then found another pitchfork and chased Grandpa Joe when we rounded the barn for the second time.

My dog, Shep, was smarter than all of us and circled the barn in the other direction and met us on the far side of the barn. I stopped suddenly and grabbed hold of Shep for protection. My dad stopped suddenly. Grandpa Joe didn't stop as quickly which resulted in his pitchfork in my dad's rear end.

Which resulted in my mom's pitchfork in Grandpa Joe's rear end. Which resulted in an even worse scolding for me. This was why my mom and Grandpa Joe didn't get along.

That's why it surprised me when Grandpa Joe moved in with us. The last few years had been hard on him. He had trouble walking caused by a lifetime of heavy farm work. He used a cane and stabilized himself while walking by holding on to furniture or supporting himself with his hand on the walls. Eventually, there was a continuous black line along our walls from his dirty hands.

One day, when he passed from the bedroom toward the kitchen, he steadied himself on the basement door. The basement door, which had been left unlatched, suddenly swung open. Grandpa Joe tumbled down the basement steps and into the basement.

When I heard Grandpa Joe yelling, I ran to the cellar door. I looked down to see him floating around in the water along with the dirt, newspapers, and scraps of clothing. There was nothing I could do to help him. I knew if I tried to pull him out, I would probably end up in the water with him.

My mom then came to the door to find out what all the noise was about. I looked up at her. From the look on her face, I could tell she was trying to decide whether to help him out or to leave him there to fend for himself.

After a few minutes, she grabbed a broom and reached it toward him. He grasped the broom handle firmly and held on as my mom pulled him from the cellar.

That's when I saw it. Grandpa Joe's pension check was sticking out from the top of his bibber overalls. If it hadn't been for that check, he would probably still be in that basement.

I bet if I had a pension check, they would have found me by now.

CHAPTER 4

AXEL AND HIS DOG

I had made an enemy and he would come back to haunt me.

Even after we moved to town, I didn't think of myself as a town boy. I felt like I didn't belong anywhere. My friends from the farm treated me like a traitor who deserted them for greener pastures. The boys from town ignored me most of the time which I preferred to the way they treated me when they did notice me.

My new friend, Pete, was a town kid. I liked him because he was about the only seven-year-old as short as me. And he wasn't like some of the other kids who acted like they were there first and knew something you didn't know and would never know.

I had lived in town for a few months when Pete told me we would have a chance to meet Axel. He was appearing at our small movie theater the day before Memorial Day. Best of all, he was giving away a new Schwinn bicycle.

I hated when the town kids teased me about my bicycle. My dad had fashioned it out of odds and ends of parts we found in the junkyard. It was good enough for the farm but didn't compare to the brand-new bicycles owned by the town kids. That's why I needed to win that new bicycle.

"We should have gotten here sooner," Pete said. "Look how long this line is."

"Yeah. All the way to the Standard gas station," I said.

"Every kid in town must be in line," he said.

"There's no way we'll all fit inside," Pete whined. "And we're near the end of the line."

We had reached Rock's Bar. We were still five stores from the movie theater.

"We might as well go home," he continued. "Only the kids up to Hruska's Hardware store will get in."

"No. Let's wait. I want to see Axel! Besides, I'm going to win that new bicycle."

"But we'll never even get in," Pete whined again.

Tom Kager drove past in a truck filled with silage. "Geez that stinks," Pete said.

"What?" I asked, hoping it wasn't me.

"Can't you smell it? The silage!" he said.

I still couldn't smell it.

The line slowly edged forward. We passed Bill's Grocery where my mom shopped and Fink and Marie's Bar where my dad usually stopped after work. When we got to the front of the First National Bank Building, which my dad claimed only the rich people used, the line suddenly came to a halt.

"See. We're not going to get in!" Pete stomped his feet and clenched his fists.

After about five minutes, the line moved again. We reached the front of the theater when the line came to a stop again. George, the owner of the theater, came up to the high school girl in the ticket booth.

"We have room for ten more."

I counted back from the door. I was number nine. Pete was ten.

"We're getting in!" I shouted.

Two kids directly behind us in line, I knew them only as Bull and Pickle, jumped in front of us. Bull because he looked like a bull and Pickle because someone decided he needed a nickname and that's the best they could come up with. They were only a couple of grades ahead of us but looked like they were old enough to be in high school.

"That's what you think!" Bull laughed.

"Hey!" Pete screamed. "We're ahead of you!"

"Not anymore!"

I darted to their left and Pete to their right. Bull elbowed Pete to the sidewalk. Pickle tripped me as I tried to pass. I looked up to see them still ahead of us.

So much for Axel and Towser and my new bicycle, I thought. After Pickle and Bull ran in through the door, I got up and turned to head for home.

"Wait!" Pete stopped me. "Look! We still might get in!"

Another usher appeared at the front door leading two young girls by the hand. He led them to a red-faced, heavy-set lady with a red babushka on her head. She grabbed each of them by an ear and led them away from the theater.

"What did you think you were doing? I told you that you couldn't see that guy who tells those dirty jokes!"

The usher guarding the door pointed at us.

"I guess you two are the last two then."

Pete and I paid and ran in.

"Hold on!" he yelled. "Take your ticket stubs. For the drawing."

We ran back for our tickets and dashed in to find a place to sit. The smell of popcorn filled the lobby.

"Let's buy some popcorn."

"We don't have time!"

Pete pulled me into the theater. George had it figured just right as we got the last two seats in the back row.

"We should have gotten two bags each since they're free," a kid in front of us said. I heard him munch on his popcorn.

We could have had free popcorn! But we were going to see Axel. In the 1950s, he had a television show, *Axel and His Dog*, which I had actually seen since we now had a television. Axel lived in a treehouse. He wore a white tee shirt with thick, horizontal black stripes and a railroad engineer's cap with the bill sticking up. His bangs were combed down, covering his forehead. Thick, white suspenders held up his baggy pants that for some reason also needed a long rope belt that hung to his knees. He would talk with a strong Norwegian accent to his puppet friends, Towser the dog or Tallulah the cat, and tell jokes between cartoons and episodes of the *Little Rascals*.

Sometimes he would read jokes sent in by kids. My Aunt Evelyn didn't think he was so funny because she heard a joke he had told on his show.

"Why did the chicken cross the road?"

"Because she's laying the farmer on the other side!"

I didn't get it. My mom thought Axel had misread the joke; it should have been laying eggs for the farmer. Aunt Evelyn thought the show should have been canceled immediately.

The lights in the theater dimmed and a spotlight shined on the curtains. Then Axel appeared through an opening.

"His stripes are red," I whispered to Pete.

"What did you expect? For him to be all black and white like on television?"

"Well, yeah," I answered.

"Yeah. I guess I did too," Pete admitted.

Towser's hairy paw reached through the curtain and rested upon Axel's shoulder. All you ever saw of Towser was his paw. I had hoped that in person we'd get to see if Towser looked like I imagined but it wasn't to be.

Axel opened with one of his Birdie jokes.

Birdie vit the yeller bill

Hopped upon my vinder sill

Cocked a shining eye and said:

What did you do when you saw your friend's home?

Run?

Bee Boop!

The kids in the theater all laughed. I did, too. But I also remembered that I almost ran home the first time I saw Pete's house, which seemed like it had more rooms than our grade school.

After Axel told a few more jokes, he held up a pair of Poll-Parrot shoes and said every boy and girl needed a pair of them. I couldn't believe he was doing a commercial. Then he introduced the movie. It was a *Little Rascals* film I had seen many times, but I didn't care. I had time to run back and get some free popcorn

After the movie, Axel appeared on the stage. Two of the ushers carried out a table full of prizes while George held a goldfish bowl filled with ticket stubs.

"The first prize we're giving away is this Davey Crockett Woodnik," Axel said. He held up the little wooden clown puppet. Pete and I watched the lucky winners march up to get their Woodniks or their Holly Days Treats or one of a dozen other toys.

Axel held up a game where you bounce a ball into a clown's face. If you got the ball in the clown's mouth it was worth a hundred points.

"The winning number is 7115," Axel announced.

I looked at my ticket stub. It was 7114. I looked over at Pete. He stared at his ticket, mouth wide open.

"Pete, is that yours?"

He couldn't answer; he could only nod.

"Go on up."

He shook his head no.

"Again, the ticket number is 7115," Axel announced.

"Go on, Pete."

He shook his head no and handed me the ticket.

It was his ticket. Why did he hand it to me? I couldn't go up on stage, in front of all these people. I was probably more afraid than Pete.

"Last call for ticket number 7115!"

I grabbed the stub and hurried down the aisle toward the front of the theater. All eyes were on me. I felt like my face must have turned beet red. I passed Pickle and Bull about three rows from the front. Bull elbowed Pickle.

"He was that kid we passed. He's got our ticket!" Bull said.

What did he mean *his* ticket? I ran up to Axel in case Bull had any ideas of taking it from me.

"What is your name, little boy?"

"Jimmie."

"Well, Jimmie. You're a lucky little boy. I hope you enjoy your game."

I hurried back to my seat, avoiding Pickle and Bull.

I had just sat down when Axel announced the next number. This was for a Pinocchio Woodnik.

"7114."

Could it be? I checked my ticket. 7114. I had the winning ticket! I had just been up there. I tried to hand my ticket to Pete, but he clutched his new clown game closer to his chest.

I got up and slowly made my way to the front, again avoiding Pickle and Bull. When I handed my ticket stub to Axel, he looked confused.

"7114. That's the ticket alright. Weren't you just up here?"

"That was me."

"My you ARE a lucky little boy. Jimmie here wanted to see Axel so bad he must have bought two tickets. This has never happened before. Didn't you already win a prize?"

"I didn't. The last one was for Pete."

"Pete? Why didn't he come down here?"

"I think he's afraid."

"How could he be afraid of Axel?"

George stepped over and whispered into Axel's ear.

"The rules are that children are allowed only one prize," Axel said. "I'm sorry but we'll have to give this prize to someone else."

I turned to leave the stage.

"Wait!"

I heard a scream from the back of the theater.

"Wait! I'm coming!"

Through the bright lights, I could see Pete running up to the stage carrying the clown game above his head.

"I did win this! Not Jimmie! See!"

Axel grabbed me by the arm and hugged me close to him.

"I guess this here Woodnik belongs to you. You *are* a lucky little boy."

He got that right.

We got back to our seats and sat back happily, thrilled that we each had won a prize. A few more Holly Days treats were awarded before Axel announced, "This next one is for the grand prize, a new Schwinn bicycle."

He drew the number from George's goldfish bowl.

"The winning number is – 7112."

"That's my ticket!" Pickle screamed, with a voice that sounded like a little girl.

I looked down at the stage to see Pickle running toward Axel. He had the winning ticket in his hand, the ticket Pete or I should have gotten. Pickle grabbed the bicycle from Axel without thanking him or George. He carried it down the steps off the stage, got on, and rode it up the aisle of the theater, running down kids that got in his way.

When he reached our row of seats, I yelled, "That bicycle should have been mine!"

Pickle stopped and gave me a dirty look.

"You better mind your own business, kid." I thought he was going to beat me up right there. He looked back up toward the stage at Axel and George. Just before he rode off, he said, "Just wait until we're alone."

CHAPTER 5

ABBER DABBER

Not winning the bicycle was only the start of it.

It happened on one of those summer days when a kid had just too much energy. Even after playing over-the-fence at Memorial Park for two hours, biking three miles out to Vasko's Creek to catch bullheads and back, we still were able to ride our bicycles up the steep hill at the other end of town. There we watched the men at Lambrecht's sawmill cut giant oaks into two-by-fours.

We were just eight kids with a summer vacation to fill. And what an odd collection of kids we were. Our parents had all sorts of jobs, from doctor to lawyer to bar owner. Our group included Bonnie, a girl, although you wouldn't know it from looking at her. The difference in our backgrounds was reflected in the way we looked. Short and fat. Tall and skinny. And everything in between.

The ride back down the hill on the west side of town rewarded us for our efforts in climbing the hill earlier. We coasted down gaining speed, the wind flowing through our hair. We swerved around slow traffic until we reached Hennes' Feed Mill where we started to wonder if we might not be able to stop at the four-way stop sign just a hundred feet away. With the scraping and grabbing of tires, we all managed to stop somewhere in the vicinity of the intersection. Out of nowhere, Pickle passed us, riding his new bicycle. He didn't even try to stop and flew on through just missing Tom Raben on his John Deere tractor.

"Chickens!" he yelled back at us from the other side, making us feel foolish for not doing something stupid. He waved for us to join him. We passed the West End Bowling Alley toward the train that was crossing Main Street a block away.

We heard Pickle counting when we reached him. "Four hundred fifty-eight. Four hundred fifty-nine. Four hundred sixty."

"Wow! Four hundred sixty cars!" said I, the ex-farm boy.

Pete said, "Don't believe him. He can't even count that high."

"Even if he takes off his shoes and socks," I added.

"Can too," Pickle answered. He moved behind me, pushing me and my bike toward the rumbling train. My feet skidded along the ground.

"Hey, stop!" I yelled.

But Pickle just shoved me closer and closer to the tracks. I was afraid I would be swallowed by the boxcars. Fortunately, the caboose passed by before that happened.

On the other side, we saw Abber Dabber. That's what everyone called him anyway. His real name was Abner Dobrovolny. But he just looked more like an Abber Dabber. He wore patched-up, dirty clothes that should have been cleaned or discarded long ago. On his short, squat body, they always seemed a couple of sizes too big. On his head, he wore a greasy, Farmall cap, always to the side of his head. Wet snuff dribbled from his mouth onto his day-old growth of gray beard.

The only thing he did all day, as far as I knew, was gather grain that had spilled along the tracks from out of passing railroad cars. He would pile sacks full of grain onto a wheelbarrow that he would push to his house on top of the steep hill. Some of the people in town complained that he was stealing and getting away with it, but others figured he was doing the town a service. Rats and other vermin would just be attracted to the trackside meal.

"Abber Dabber!" Pickle yelled as he rode his bike toward him, just missing him at the last second. Soon, we were all circling Abber Dabber like Indians surrounding a covered wagon.

"Whatcha want boys?" he said, calmly.

"Abber Dabber! Abber Dabber!" We all shouted. It reached a high-pitched crescendo. We began the Indian war-whoop. Finally, Abber Dabber moved forward, tired of our little game. Pickle had another idea. He rode directly in front of him blocking his path. That's when Abber Dabber's strong, firm hand grabbed the handlebars of Pickle's bike, causing it to come to an abrupt stop. Pickle flew over the bars. He landed face-first on the graveled road. When he came up for air, I saw blood through the dirt on his face, hands, and knees. He looked like he wanted to cry but couldn't in front of us. Yet, he was unable to prevent a few sobs from escaping his gaping mouth.

The rest of us fell silent when Mrs. Tyler, an eighth-grade teacher, stopped her car near the tracks.

"What happened here?" she screamed.

Pickle said, "Abber Dabber knocked me off my bike, for no reason!"

"Is this true?" she asked.

No one answered. Not even Abber Dabber who slowly moved back to his wheelbarrow full of grain that had overturned and spilled onto the tracks. Mrs. Tyler followed on his heels, much like the owner of a disobedient puppy.

"From now on it would behoove you to refrain from such activity or I shall have to report you to the authorities. Do you understand?"

"Yes Ma'am," he replied. Mrs. Tyler turned her attention to Pickle who accepted the nursing she was administering like a hero returning from the wars.

"Pickle started it," I blurted out.

Pickle broke away from Mrs. Tyler and headed toward me.

"Stop right there. It doesn't matter who started it."

She helped him and his bicycle into her car and drove him home. The rest of us slowly crept away, gathering near a bench in the park a block away.

"I guess you showed him. Huh, Jimmie?" Mike said after a long silence.

"Shut up!" I answered, not knowing if he was referring to Pickle or Abber Dabber. I looked back at Abber Dabber slowly putting his grain back into his wheelbarrow. I didn't feel like I *showed* anyone anything. Instead, I felt like I did when my little kitten, Snowball, died.

"What's with you, Jimmie?" Mike said. "Pickle will never forget about this. The next time he sees you…"

"Shut up, Mike," Bonnie said. "Don't you know when to shut up?"

With that, Mike peeled away on his bike. Slowly we went our separate ways.

Thoughts raced through my mind but none of them made any sense. Yes, Pickle started it and I said he had. But I felt worse because I joined in.

I caught up with Abber Dabber at the foot of the steep hill. I came to a skidding halt, ditching my bike in the tall weeds next to Dorn's yard. I marched to the front of Abber Dabber's wheelbarrow.

"Leave me alone!" he said. "I don't want no trouble."

I didn't answer. I just grabbed the handles of his wheelbarrow.

"Let me help you," I said.

Together we pushed the wheelbarrow up the hill and into Abber Dabber's cluttered front yard.

CHAPTER 6

THE FROG PRINCE

I would rather be in school.

Sister Florida was going to be our teacher again, this time for the fifth grade. Did she miss us that much? She found a new way to make our lives a little more miserable. Our class was going to put on a play. It was going to be fun, she said. We would learn a lot, she said. We'd become better friends with our classmates, she said.

Tommy heard that and he figured it would just be a lot of hard work, he wouldn't learn anything, and he would end up hating his classmates.

"I'm not getting up in front of everybody and make a fool of myself."

But he was so good at it, I thought.

Sister Florida glided up and down the aisle handing out copies of the play to each student. I looked at the cover when she placed it on my desk. It was *The Frog Prince*.

"Who gets what parts?" Barb asked.

Sister Florida stood in front of the class with her arms crossed over her chest.

"I would like each of you to read the play. There is a part for each of you. Please write down on a piece of paper your top three choices of a role you would like to play and hand it in to me tomorrow morning. I will then assign each student a part."

I immediately looked for the three parts with the fewest lines. There were two parts with no lines at all!

"I'm going to be the princess," Barb announced.

That didn't surprise me. She probably thought she could take every part and act out the whole play by herself.

"And if all the boys sign up for the roles with no lines," Sister Florida said, "I will assign them as I see fit."

Was she looking at me?

I looked through the play more closely.

There was the frog. No. Too many lines.

There was the princess. No. A girl's part and too many lines.

The king. No. Too many lines and a beard.

Also out were the two sisters, handmaiden, queen, waitresses, and the queen's court.

The trees, the rocks, the cook, the knights, and the guards all had no lines.

Then I found it. The prince's servant, Faithful Henry.

He had only one line.

'Your carriage awaits.'

I didn't know what it meant but I was pretty sure I could remember it.

One of the guards, who had three lines, was my second choice. I liked him because he always let the frog into the castle.

The king was my last choice. He had a lot of lines, but he was nice to the frog and made the princess do what she had promised to do.

The next day I had forgotten about the play when Sister Florida remembered not to forget. Just before the final bell, she stood in front of the class. She pulled a sheet of paper somewhere out of her habit. She probably even had a chicken or rabbit hidden up her sleeve.

"God does not always give us what we want. Sometimes He gives us that which makes us stronger." She looked about the room with that all-knowing face that made me believe in every word she said.

"Therefore, each of you did not receive his or her first choice in the play. That means, I am sorry to say since she would have made the perfect princess, Barb will play the part of the queen."

I was sure I heard Barb whimper. When I turned to look at her, she had her head buried in her arms on the desk.

"Howard will play the servant, Faithful Henry."

Okay. If not the servant, the guard. The guard would be all right.

"Thomas will play a guard."

Why Tommy? But maybe there were other guards.

"And James will play the king."

I dug my copy of the play out of my desk and counted the King's lines. Twenty-three lines. Twenty-three! How was I ever going to remember that many lines? Sister Florida said God was just trying to make me stronger, but I didn't really want to be that strong.

"One more thing," Sister Florida said through the rustle of paper. "This year we are going to get the parents involved. I am sure your parents will be more than happy to make each of your costumes."

She didn't know my mother.

"A king," my mom said. "Why did you have to go and be a king? What's wrong with being something I know how to make?"

"Like a servant?"

"Yes. A servant I could do easy."

"Maybe you could talk to Sister Florida," I said.

I saw fear in her eyes like when she had my grandma and aunts over for company and had to get the house spic and span.

"Maybe I can do a king. What does a king look like? What does a king wear anyway?"

"I know he's got a beard. And a crown."

The class rehearsed the play for an hour each day. I was getting some of my lines almost right. The worst part was remembering where and what you were supposed to be doing on stage. It seemed like we were always tripping and bumping into each other.

The princess, played by Darlene, at one point sits on the king's lap. I was uncomfortable with her doing that and I think Darlene was as well.

She just couldn't get it right for Sister Florida. It didn't help that she was almost twice as big as me. Tommy said it looked like a cow trying to sit on a chicken. Most of the time he said it looked like I, the king, wasn't even under there.

Sister Florida finally decided, in order to save the king's life, the princess could just sit on her own chair.

I wondered what would happen later on when Pete, the frog, hops onto the princess's lap.

I was glad I wasn't the frog. I guess there are worse things than being a king.

Then we got to rehearse in the auditorium on the real stage. It was much bigger than our practice stage in front of the classroom. We still stood as close to each other as when we had rehearsed, occupying a tiny area near the back. Sister Florida finally spread us out, so we no longer were bumping into each other.

I looked out at the empty chairs that would be filled with grownups and students just waiting for me to make a mistake or forget a line.

At home, my family was busy making a king's costume. My dad tried to make a crown out of a coffee can. The points on the crown were too sharp, it was too small, and it was red with the name *Folgers* across the front.

Uncle Vencil made another crown. He took one of my good caps apart to help him get the size right. But I didn't mind. It fit. I don't know what he made it out of, but it was light. After he painted it gold, it looked exactly like the one in the book.

For the king's robe, my mom got a purple robe from Aunt Rose which was too big until my mom hemmed it. It smelled like Aunt Rose's perfume and had frilly white cuffs on the sleeves until I made my mom remove them.

Uncle John cut off part of his horse's tail for a beard. He figured Daisy wouldn't miss it. It scratched my face, but my mom said I would just have to put up with it.

When I put the entire costume on, everyone said that I sort of looked like a king. But I smelled like a painted horse wearing perfume.

I tried to get my dad to read the frog's lines, but he said he wasn't doing it right. I thought he was but there was no changing his mind.

So, Uncle Vencil rehearsed the frog parts with me.

My mom was having fun playing the queen. I practiced my lines over and over with her.

There was one line with the queen I just seemed to get wrong every time.

The queen says, "The princess has promised to let the frog spend the night in the castle. What is our daughter to do?"

Then I, the king, answer, "A promise is a promise. And the princess must keep her promise to the frog."

I kept mixing the words around and putting the princess where the promise was supposed to be.

The night before the play, I couldn't sleep and when I did, I had nightmares about forgetting my lines. I knew what I had to do.

I told Sister Florida I was quitting, and she could find someone else to be her king.

She sat me down and looked me in the eye.

"James, you cannot quit."

"But I can't remember my lines."

"James, you may think you'll forget your lines. But when you are on stage, you are the king. How could the king himself forget what he has to say?"

She had me there.

The night of the play, I looked out at the audience. All those people. It was enough to make anyone, even the king forget what he had to say.

Then I saw my family sitting about four rows from the stage. Even Ron, although he didn't look very happy to be there.

I couldn't back out with all of them expecting me to be the king.

And when the play started, I forgot I was Jimmie. I was the king.

Everything was going well until it got to the part with the queen that I always mixed up.

That's when the queen, Barb, must have forgotten her line. She could memorize our whole fifth-grade history book, but she forgot one of her three simple lines. I had to wonder if she did it on purpose.

Sister Florida tried to whisper the line to Barb. But it just sounded like whispering to me. Time stopped on the stage. Silence filled the auditorium.

Then I heard a voice from the audience. "The princess has promised to let the frog spend the night in the castle. What is our daughter to do?"

I turned to see my mom standing at her seat. Then her face turned red in embarrassment before she sat down.

I remembered my line.

CHAPTER 7

WHY THE ACCORDION

I would even rather be in school in front of class.

Barb stood in front of Sister Florida's classroom reciting Lincoln's Gettysburg Address. She had the whole speech memorized! At least the other kids had to read from a book or handwritten pages. But Barb had it memorized. What a showoff. I had always liked Barb, but I didn't like her so much right now.

I was about the only kid in class who hadn't 'performed' for the fifth-grade class. Sister Florida thought it would be good for each student to get up in front of the class. I didn't think it was so good. I knew I would be nervous with everyone staring at me. I knew I would sweat so much my shirt would be drenched. I knew everyone would laugh at me.

"...shall not perish from the earth."

Barb had just finished the Gettysburg Address. Sister Florida swooped toward her, applauding and grinning from ear to ear, except you couldn't see her ears because they were covered by her habit. She hugged Barb so hard I could hear the breath crushed out of her from the back row.

"That was excellent. By far the best performance so far. I'm so proud of you," Sister Florida announced to the class. "But just remember, students. God just wants you to do your best. That's all He asks."

However, I could tell Sister Florida was asking for more. She was almost glowing. If she would have had the power, I was sure she would have made Barb a saint right then and there in front of the whole class.

Barb paraded down the aisle and sat in the seat next to me. She turned and looked down her nose at me.

"So, what are you going to do, Jimmie?"

"Uh. I don't know."

"That's right, Jimmie," she said turning away. "You can't do anything special."

I didn't like Barb anymore. I could do things, but they weren't things you could do in front of the class.

I could milk a cow, but Sister Florida wouldn't let me do that in front of the class, even if I could fit a cow through the doorway.

Sister Florida called Mike's name. He walked to the front of the class. He didn't want to be there. I could tell from the look on his face. He opened his mouth, but nothing came out. For about thirty seconds, he just stood there.

"You may start any time now, Michael," Sister Florida said.

Mike nodded his head. He lifted his piece of paper and started to read.

"Four scores and seven years ago..."

He had the bad luck of choosing the same reading as Barb. He had to read it from his paper and hadn't memorized it as Barb had. And already he had made a mistake.

Then the strangest thing happened. Sister Florida stopped him.

"Michael. That's the Gettysburg Address. Yesterday you announced that you would sing 'America the Beautiful' for us, and I was looking forward to that. We are not allowed to change, are we?"

Mike stammered a bit. "No. But I can't sing it."

"What do you mean, you can't? There is no such thing as can't."

Maybe for Sister Florida, there was no can't. But there was for me.

"You may sit down now. Tomorrow you will perform 'America the Beautiful' for the class, and it will be beautiful, I am sure. Now James, what will you do for us tomorrow?"

That's me, I realized. My mind raced. Cows. Fishing. Driving a tractor. Throwing a baseball. None of those would work.

"James?"

"The Gettysburg Address," I blurted out.

"Ah, no, James. That's already been done. One too many times, in fact."

Then it came out, from out of nowhere. "I'm going to play the 'Mosquito Polka' on the accordion."

Why had I said that? I had never played an accordion before. I didn't even have an accordion.

But my grandpa had one. He kept it in a closet in his back bedroom. I knew for sure that my dad couldn't afford to buy me one and even if he could, where would they find one on such short notice. No, I decided, I would just borrow Grandpa Joe's accordion and learn to play some song on it. Something that Sister Florida might think was the 'Mosquito Polka' if she didn't know the song.

That night while everyone was sleeping, I crept upstairs to Grandpa Joe's room. The accordion was in a huge black case at the bottom of the closet. It was bigger than I had remembered. It took both of my hands and a lot of tugging just to get it out of the closet.

I wasn't able to carry it. I had to lift and set it down every step down the staircase to my room. By the time I reached my room, my shirt and pants were drenched. I was exhausted. It was too late to learn a song on the accordion. Not only that, but I would also wake the whole house playing just one note.

The next day I had to sneak the accordion out the back door of our house. I dragged the accordion case through the streets to school and into the classroom.

If Sister Florida wanted me to play, that's what I would do, somehow.

Mike was called to the front of the classroom. This time he did sing 'America the Beautiful' without a piano to help him, and it actually was pretty good.

This made me more confident. If Mike could do it, maybe I could too.

When Sister Florida called my name, I slowly made my way to the front of the class with the accordion.

Sister Florida moved a chair from near her desk for me. I opened the case and picked up the accordion. It was shiny and red with white and black keys. And it was much bigger than I had remembered.

Somehow, I managed to take it out of the case and strap it on as I sat down on the chair.

I reached around the accordion, barely able to even touch any of the keys. I hit one key as I pushed on the bellows. The sound of a sick calf came out of the accordion.

"James! Stop!"

"Yes, Sister."

"You don't know how to play the accordion, do you?"

"Why do you say that?"

"For one thing. You have it on upside down."

CHAPTER 8

TREASURE ISLAND

Along one wall of the bank, there is a bookshelf filled with books. I opened a few of them but I couldn't understand most of the words. And the subject matter didn't interest me. What is 'Financial Diversification' anyway? I read a few paragraphs and from the words I could understand, it was about spending money on different things. Didn't most people do that anyway?

Sister Florida's new assignment was a book report. Each member of our class had to read a book. Not only that, but we also had to go to the town library to get the book. Part of the assignment was to read a chapter on libraries, which I hadn't done since I had forgotten the textbook at school. I was assigned *Treasure Island*. I had no idea what it was about, but I was pretty sure it wasn't about farming in Minnesota since there were no treasures or islands on farms.

The town library was located in the basement of Vevea's Grocery Store. I opened the door at the side of the building and walked into the entryway. The worn, wooden steps downstairs were dimly lit, probably by the original bulb.

I walked down to the musty-smelling basement, not sure what to expect. The first thing I saw was the librarian. I figured it had to be her since she sat at a desk with a nameplate that said, LIBRARIAN: MRS. MAKISKA. She was an old, heavy-set lady of about forty wearing a flowered, red and yellow dress a little too small for her. When I reached the green and white tiled library floor, I saw shelves and shelves of books illuminated by bright fluorescent lights. One light flickered over a shelf of books labeled, FICTION T. I found it right away! *Treasure Island* had to be on this shelf.

I went down the aisle to where the Ts started. But none of the books started with TREASURE. Did Mrs. Makiska put the book in the wrong place? Finally, I decided I had to ask her where the book was. That was the last thing I wanted to do. I walked up to her like I was walking to the front of our class to talk to Sister Florida.

"Where can I find *Treasure Island*?"

She looked over her glasses at me.

"Did you look in the card catalog?"

"No."

Why would the book be in there, I wondered?

"If you would have, you would have found it was written by Robert Louis Stevenson. So, it would be in the FICTION section under S."

I was close. But why wouldn't you put the books on the shelves by title? By the author didn't make any sense to me. I went back to the same shelf and searched through the books. Of course, it was at the end of the top shelf. There was no way I could reach it. I jumped a few times, but I didn't come close to it.

I placed my foot on the first shelf and stepped up to reach for the book. I jumped down quickly when I felt the shelf teetering toward me. I pictured myself buried under a pile of books. When Sister Florida gave us this assignment, the whole class had groaned. She said it wouldn't kill us to write a book report. I had almost proved her wrong.

"Ahem!" That was Mrs. Makiska. She had a stern look on her face. She pointed to a three-step stool in the corner. I slid it over to the shelf and stepped up and grabbed *Treasure Island*.

After I moved the stool back into the corner, I started out the door with my book. Again, I heard the 'ahem' from Mrs. Makiska.

"Where are you going with that book, young man?"

"Ah, home?"

"Not until you check it out."

"Check it out?"

She waved me to her desk. Again, I made the long 'teacher's' walk.

"You must give me your library card so I can sign the book out to you and let you know when it is due back."

"I don't have one. Does that mean I can't take the book? I have to do a book report and…"

"That's okay. I can issue you a card. What is your name?"

After I told her my name she asked, "Do you have any proof of that? So, I can be sure you are who you say you are."

"No. But I'm me. Why would anyone pretend to be me?"

"Do you have any school papers with your name?"

"Everything is at home."

I heard footsteps coming down the stairs. When I turned, I saw it was Abber Dabber. I was shocked to see him.

"Mr. Dobrovolny? You're in the library?"

"Yes, Jimmie. Why does that surprise you? I've been reading since I was younger than you."

Mrs. Makiska said, "Mr. Dobrovolny. You know James?"

"Why, sure. His father and I practically grew up together."

"You did?" I said. "I didn't know that."

"We played on the Plum Creek Plums together."

"Plums?" Mrs. Makiska said.

"Wasn't my idea," Abber Dabber laughed.

Mrs. Makiska slid her glasses on and said, "Well, James. I think I can issue you a card."

While I answered her questions, Abber Dabber picked up the book I was going to check out.

"*Treasure Island* is one of my favorite books. Let me see how many times I've read it."

I wondered how he was going to find that out. He opened the front cover and pulled a card from an envelope glued to the first page.

"Four times. See."

He showed the card to me. He pointed out each time his name was signed on the card and the dates he had checked the book out.

"You should know all this already, James," Mrs. Makiska said.

"I guess I should have read that chapter Sister Florida gave us."

"I should make you go home and read the chapter before I let you sign out the book."

"But I left it at school."

She thought it over for a while and finally said, "Here's your library card. Just sign and date the card from the book."

"Thank you, Mrs. Makiska."

As I signed, I wondered how many times my name would appear on that card or other books in the library. Would I ever catch up with Abber Dabber? I grabbed the book and turned and walked over to Abber Dabber at the card catalog.

"Thank you," I said. "Can I ask you something? Will you show me how to use that?"

"The card catalog? Sure."

When he explained it, it was easy. He taught me the Dewey Decimal System. He knew everything about the library.

"Thank you, Mr. Dobrovolny. Now I won't have to read that chapter Sister Florida assigned."

"James, I suggest you read that chapter," Mrs. Makiska said.

That was when I started to think Mrs. Makiska was Sister Florida in disguise.

"Mr. Dobrovolny, can I find out about the NFO? My dad won't tell me anything about it."

"Sure."

He walked me through the process of finding a magazine with an article about the NFO in Minnesota.

"Maybe now I can find out why farmers think they can come out ahead by spilling their milk on the ground."

I grabbed the magazine and started up the steps.

"Just a minute, young man."

Mrs. Makiska was looking over her glasses at me again.

"Oh, that's right. I have to sign it out."

"No, James. Magazines cannot leave the library."

"They can't?"

"No, James. You can sit at that table and read it if you'd like."

I took a seat and started to read the article. Right there in the first sentence was a word I didn't know.

"What does anarchy mean, Mr. Dobrovolny?"

"It means…"

"Abner, excuse me. James, we could tell you, but it would be better if you looked it up yourself. The dictionary is over there in the reference section."

I figured it would be better if she had just told me, but I brought the huge book back to the table and looked up the definition. On the cover, in large capital letters were the unnecessary words, NOT TO BE REMOVED FROM THE LIBRARY. Of course not. It was too heavy to carry out.

I looked up to see Mrs. Makiska putting up a poster titled, FUN AT THE LIBRARY.

I learned a couple of things about the library that day. One thing was that the library had more rules than Sister Florida and the Catholic Church. Another was that the library wasn't fun unless you were Mrs. Makiska. And there was no anarchy in her library.

CHAPTER 9

CZECH CHOW MEIN

Hiding in a bank makes a person thirsty. It's a good thing there was a water fountain. I was hungry until I found a box of chocolates on one of the desks. I ate all the pieces except one. I did leave all the wrappers, though.

Just before Christmas, the Monsignor at our school decided to try something different. Instead of holding Mass the first thing each morning, he held Mass for the students just before lunch. I asked Sister Florida why he did this. She said it was God's will. I wondered why God would care when we had lunch. I thought of two other reasons. One was that the Monsignor didn't want to get up so early to say Mass. The other was more likely. Too many kids showed up late for school and skipped the Mass.

Maybe it could have been both.

Each day at eleven in the morning, we were marched from the school to the Church in single file and genuflected our way into the pews. The nuns monitored this closely, making sure our knees touched the floor when we genuflected, that our backs were straight when we knelt at the pews, and that our rear ends weren't resting on the seats.

The Masses were in Latin, which made no sense to me. For all I knew, I was promising God I would become a priest and didn't know it. I asked why Mass was held in Latin and she said it was God's will. I figured it was because God only understood Latin.

Once Mass started, it never seemed to stop. Just when I thought it would end, the Monsignor would throw in a new prayer or two at the end. I wouldn't have minded it if Mass was the first thing in the morning. It would mean less time in the classroom. Since my breakfast, as my mom would say, wouldn't keep a bird alive, I was starving by the time noon arrived.

To make it even worse, the cafeteria was in the Church basement. By the middle of Mass, I could smell whatever meal the Czech ladies were making for lunch. By the end of Mass, the aroma filled the Church and my mind. Instead of praying for starving children in Africa, I was praying for a starving kid in that Church.

When Mass would finally end, the children lined up by classes to march downstairs for lunch, with grade one going first. That meant our class was toward the end of the line. I watched as the line slowly moved toward the front of the cafeteria. It seemed when I was in that Catholic school, I was always in a line. Even to the bathroom.

Why had I thought of that? I suddenly had to go to the bathroom. I had a dilemma. I could step out of line to go and return to the end of the line. Or stay in line and suffer an embarrassing situation.

So later, I found myself at the end of the line. When I finally reached the Czech lady, she spooned out the remaining chunk of lunch onto my tray. It was chow mein.

It was a good thing I was hungry. Czech ladies usually made great meals. But chow mein wasn't one of them. I grabbed a bowl of green jello with peaches in it and hurried to finish my meal before noon recess.

On most days, I enjoyed recess. But that day, it was snowing and freezing outside. Most kids had heavy parkas and warm boots. But all my coats and boots still smelled like the farm. I refused to wear them to school.

Instead, I just wore a light jacket and a baseball cap. Perfect for a ballgame but not a winter recess.

I tried running around the schoolyard to get warm. But that only made me colder. I looked at the nuns standing in the classroom windows. They seemed to be looking at me, enjoying my discomfort. They probably figured it was God's will.

I decided to run around the Church so they wouldn't see me. When I turned the far corner, I felt a blast of warm air. I stopped next to an exhaust vent from the cafeteria. Warmth. It smelled like chow mein. I knew if I stood under the vent for the rest of the noon recess, I would smell like chow mein. I didn't care. I was warm.

Then I felt a tap on my shoulder. I turned to see Sister Benedict.

"I saw you run behind the Church. I wondered where you had gone," she said.

"I was cold. Then I found this warm spot here," I said.

"You should be playing with the other children," she said. "It is healthy for you to play outside."

Is that why you and the other nuns are inside where it's warm? I thought it but didn't say it.

Instead, I said, "Yes, Sister."

"Why are you standing here, away from all the others?" she asked.

I had already told her this was a warm spot. So, I tried an answer that always seemed to work.

"Because it was God's will," I answered.

I spent the rest of noon recess inside. Standing in a corner. But I was warm.

CHAPTER 10

POLIO

Yes, I was trapped in a bank, but it could be worse. At least, I could move around. At least, I could walk.

My mom told me I wasn't allowed to play with Kenny. I hadn't seen him since last spring. He hadn't been to school for two months and no one knew why. At least, no one knew anything they would tell me.

When I told my folks I wanted to see him anyway, they told me not to visit him. When I asked why, they responded with their usual grownup answer. Because we said so.

My classmates had a lot of ideas about what was going on.

Dan knew why Kenny wasn't in school. He was telling everyone that Kenny was so dumb he had flunked every subject and the nuns didn't want any stupid kids in school.

I knew Kenny wasn't dumb. He got the best grades of any boy in class and even some of the girls.

Dan said the nuns didn't like kids who flunked religion. They would be sinners for the rest of their lives. Just being around them would make other kids sinners.

"But what about Confession?" I asked. "Wasn't that what Confession was for?"

Dan said kids who flunked religion couldn't go to Confession and would go to Hell.

Gloria thought Kenny wasn't in our class because he now was going to the public school. I didn't know what a public school was. When I asked her, she said it was a school for people who weren't Catholic and would go to Hell.

Howie heard Kenny was kicked out of school because he was supposed to study to become a priest and refused. I didn't know you had to study to be a priest. I didn't even realize that they took normal kids like Kenny. I tried to picture him standing up in the pulpit telling everyone how evil they were. Howie said the nuns told Kenny he had the calling and if he didn't become a priest, he would go to Hell.

I had heard three reasons why Kenny wasn't in school. They all ended up with Kenny going to Hell. So, I had to find out for myself.

Kenny's mom answered the door when I got there. At first, she looked surprised to see me. Then almost a little angry. She tightened her housecoat, using her left hand to close it around her neck. Usually, she was quite cheerful and full of energy; now it looked like it was all she could do to keep her eyes open.

"Jimmie! You shouldn't be here!" she snapped at me.

"I came to see Kenny. I ran right over after school."

A pained look appeared on her face. She stood there silently for a while; her eyes squinted closed. She threw her head back and took in a deep breath.

"I'm sorry but you have to go."

"But I want to see Kenny. Is he here?"

"Yes, but he can't have visitors now."

She reached for the door and started to close it on me.

"Why not? Please. I won't stay long."

I barely got that last sentence out before she slammed the door on me.

That's why I decided to hide in the bushes outside Kenny's house. If his mom didn't want me to visit Kenny, I would have to wait until I was sure she left the house. I could then sneak in when no one was around and find out for myself why Kenny wouldn't see me. At least, that was the plan.

It was the plan for three hours. During this time, I tried to think of reasons why Kenny wouldn't see me. I hadn't done anything to him to make him mad at me. I didn't think I had.

It could have been something he thought I had done. Like the time I was so mad at Ron for taking my new baseball glove and not giving it back. Two days later I remembered that I had tied a baseball inside the glove with baling twine to form a perfect pocket and stuffed the glove under my mattress. I remembered because my mom found it while changing my sheets.

Or maybe Dan told Kenny some lie about me, and Kenny believed him. Dan was always doing that. Even about himself. Like the story about him being Crazy Horse's grandson. He didn't even look like an Indian.

Then it got dark. And it started to rain. I had just assumed Kenny's mom would leave the house. She would have to leave the house some time, wouldn't she?

I gave up and went home.

I waited outside in the bushes every day for almost a week. And she hadn't left the house. That's when it hit me. Church! On Sunday! Both of Kenny's parents never missed Church. That meant I wouldn't even have to wait in the bushes.

When I got to his house on Sunday, I checked to make sure Kenny's Dad's car wasn't in the driveway. I tiptoed up the porch steps and slowly opened the front door and snuck inside. Music from a radio or record player could be heard coming from the direction of Kenny's room upstairs.

Slowly, I crept up the stairway, looking behind me every step to make sure no one was coming up from the rear. I got to the top of the stairs just as I heard a lady's voice in Kenny's room.

"Just get some rest now. You hear?"

I ducked into a closet outside Kenny's room before the lady exited his room. When I peeked out through the crack in the door, I saw a heavy-set woman, dressed entirely in white like the nurse at our school. She made her way downstairs with an empty food tray. After I was sure she was gone, I crept into Kenny's room. He was sitting in a wheelchair and wrapped in a blanket. He looked pale and thin. Heavy braces covered his legs.

"What are you doing here?" he whispered when he saw me.

"I came to see you."

"You shouldn't have come." He paused, looking down. "I can't walk."

"Well, how can you with those big things on your legs?" I said.

"The doctor said I need them. I don't have enough strength in my legs to hold me up."

"How can that be? Just a few months ago you could easily outrun me."

"Not anymore. I just woke up one morning and I couldn't move my legs. The doctor thinks it's polio."

"What is that? Something you ate?"

"No, it's something you catch. Like a cold or flu."

If I got polio, I had only myself to blame. It would be my fault for coming to see him. That's why no one wanted me to see him.

"I was supposed to get a shot for it, so I wouldn't get it," Kenny said. "But I was sick with a cold that day."

"So, you got polio because you had a cold."

"Yeah, I guess," Kenny said. "It's a good thing you got vaccinated for it."

I hadn't gotten vaccinated for it, either. The day they were making all the kids at school get those shots, I didn't know what they were for. I was afraid and hid in the boy's bathroom until the school let out. It might have hurt a little, but now I would rather have that shot than what Kenny had.

"Does it hurt?" I asked.

"No, mostly my legs feel weak."

"When are you going to get better?"

"The doctor doesn't know. Maybe never."

"Never! That can't be right."

Tears flowed down my cheeks. I tried to stop them, to make myself brave for Kenny. But I couldn't even be brave for myself.

"You know, you're the only friend who has come to see me," Kenny said.

After he said that, I knew I had to hug him and hold him close. The only person I had ever hugged before was my mother. It would be stupid to hug someone with polio. But my stupid foot took a step toward him.

"Stop!" Kenny said.

That didn't stop me.

"Stop right there, young boy," the nurse yelled. "What are you doing in here?"

That stopped me.

"Get out of here this instant."

My legs quickly carried me down the stairs and out of the house. My legs were still strong. I ran all the way home, thinking of Kenny in that wheelchair. I was afraid for him and afraid for myself. I couldn't get polio from just looking at Kenny. Or could I?

CHAPTER 11

POLIO, TOO

I was really sick. The kind of sick you get when you have the flu, only worse. I had a fever. I had the chills. I was throwing up. I had the runs. My stomach ached. My eyes hurt so much I thought they would explode. I was so weak I couldn't get out of bed. Everything hurt so much I thought I was dying. Maybe I was.

I wondered what dying was like. Was it nothing? Or was it like the nuns said? Angels with wings. Satan and gnashing and grinding of teeth. Whatever it was, it had to be better than this.

It seemed like my mom woke me up every few minutes and tried to spoon chicken soup into me, most of which came out as quickly as it went in. Each time before she left, she would slather my chest with Vick's VapoRub, dipping the white salve out of the dark blue jar with her fingers. If Vick's was supposed to make me feel better, it wasn't working and seemed to have entirely the opposite effect.

Then with a worried look, she would feel my forehead to check if the fever had gone down. Only her loving kiss on my forehead before she left seemed to help.

After she left, I would work myself into a deep sleep filled with dreams that made me more tired for having dreamt them. Dreams about horrifying creatures I had no name for but lived in the reality of my nightmares only to cause me as much pain in my sleep as my sickness caused me when I was awake. Even when I knew I was dreaming, they wouldn't let me escape and awaken.

When I finally woke up, I was soaked in sweat, throwing up the nothing inside me there was to throw up. Day and night blended together. People appeared and disappeared from my room as if by magic. At times I wondered who these people were at my bedside, struggling to put names to the faces only to realize minutes later that yes, that was Vencil! You're Uncle John! Mom! How could I forget my mom?

Then one night there was a man I couldn't put a name to. A man who made me open my mouth and held my tongue down with a Popsicle stick. He looked into my ears and up my nose. He felt around my neck and pressed on my stomach.

"Does that hurt, Jimmie?"

I couldn't answer. I could only scream in pain. Of course, it hurt. What did he think? I finally remembered he was the town doctor. Doc Sladek.

"Please raise your arms for me, Jimmie."

With great effort, I lifted my arms high in the air but saw them move only about an inch off the bed.

"Now your legs, Jimmie. Can you move your legs?"

Of course, I could. I looked down as I moved my legs. But even with all my strength, I couldn't make them move. I turned to see the frightened look on my mom's face before she turned away from me.

"Keep trying, Jimmie," my dad encouraged, his hand on my shoulder. I had always done what he had wanted before. But no matter how hard I tried, my legs wouldn't move.

Everyone moved away from the bed to a far corner of the room and spoke in whispers, leaving me to hold back my sobs, straining to hear what they were saying. I heard only one word. Polio.

CHAPTER 12

RAW ONIONS AND HAMBURGER

I had been awake all night. If only I could sleep.

Doc Sladek was a huge man about the size of my Uncle John and my dad put together. I never liked him getting close to me because he smelled like raw onions and beer. For lunch, he would eat raw onions and raw hamburger at the Corner Bar and wash them down with a few glasses of beer.

He walked over to me with a giant needle in his hands. That was the other reason I didn't want him getting close to me. I knew what was next and I tried not to think about it. Instead, I thought of my friend, Kenny, and his horrible wheelchair which was worse. Would the same thing happen to me? Was this happening to me because I went to see him that day? I didn't even feel it when the doctor gave me the shot.

"This will help you sleep," Doc Sladek said in a gentle voice. And it did.

When I woke up, it was light outside, and I was feeling much better. I didn't feel like throwing up and I didn't have a fever. Mostly I felt weak and hungry, and I had to pee. I threw off my covers and swung my legs onto the floor. Except when I looked down, they were still in the bed. Then I remembered.

"Mom! Mom!" I cried out. "Mom! Help!"

Within seconds, my mom was by my bed. So was everyone else. Even Ron.

"It's okay, Jimmie. It's okay."

"No, Mom. I can't move my legs."

"It'll be okay, Jimmie. Don't cry."

But I wasn't crying. I was too scared to cry. I could only think of the rest of my life in this bed. No more baseball. No more ice skating. No more biking. I closed my eyes and remembered fetching the cows with Shep back on the farm. Running after them through the woods trying to keep up with them, the wind blowing through my hair, ducking to avoid branches, and jumping to avoid cowpies. When I opened my eyes, I was still on the bed. And my legs wouldn't move.

"Here," my mom said, handing me two pills. "Doc Sladek said these would make you sleep." And they did.

When I woke up, my mom was still sitting by my bed. Her eyes were red like she had been crying.

"How are you feeling, Jimmie?"

"Fine. Better. I think."

She pulled back the covers.

"Can you move your legs?"

I tried but when I looked down, they weren't moving.

"I'm going to try something."

She stood up and bent over my legs. Her strong hands grasped one of my legs, the huge muscles in her arms bulging. Muscles made strong from the endless hours of milking cows by hand. She began to knead my legs, just like I had seen her do when she kneaded the bread dough in the kitchen.

"Let me know if it hurts."

But it didn't hurt. I wished that it would have but I couldn't feel anything at all. I looked down at my lifeless, worthless leg which didn't feel like a part of me. It was no use to me. It might as well have belonged to someone else.

I looked up at the green and white teapot clock, which used to be our kitchen clock until my dad bought mom a new one for Christmas. The second hand moved slowly across from its handle around to its spout. The minute hand seemed to be stuck on eleven and the hour hand stuck on seven.

The next thing I knew I was asleep. When I woke up again, it was after nine o'clock. My mom was still working on my legs. I assumed she had been doing this the entire time I had been sleeping. Her hair was wet and perspiration was running down her face.

Day turned into night. I would drift in and out. Whenever I would open my eyes, I would see my mom squeezing the muscles in my thighs or calves. Sometimes Aunt Mara or my dad would be helping. But always my mom.

"You need to get some sleep," Aunt Mara finally said to her.

"I can't sleep. You know that."

"At least rest, then."

My mom just shook her head no.

I was just about to drift off to sleep again when it hit me. I felt a sharp pain in the calf of my right leg.

"Yeoww!" I screamed. My mom released her grip on my leg.

"What? Something hurt?" she asked.

I nodded yes and pointed to my calf.

"Try and move your legs. See if they move."

I tried. But when I looked down at my legs, they weren't moving.

"Jimmie!" my mom said. I could hear the excitement in her voice. "They moved. The toes on your right foot moved."

"They did?"

"Yes, Jimmie. They did." Her strong hands, which had been tirelessly working my legs, tenderly touched my face. "They did."

She bent over and went to work again, her fingers trying to put life back into my legs.

I don't know how long I had been asleep. When I awoke, it was dark outside. Doc Sladek bent over me.

"Open wide."

He stuck a thermometer under my tongue, a little too rough as far as I was concerned. It almost poked a hole where my tongue met with the bottom of my mouth.

"And you say his foot hasn't moved since?"

"Just that once."

I couldn't help but see her worried look.

Doc Sladek removed the thermometer and checked the temperature. If it was too high, too low, or normal, he didn't bother to let anyone else know.

"Just that once."

"Yes. But not again after that. Is that bad?"

"It's bad but it could be worse."

Sure, it could be worse. I could be dead.

"Will I ever walk again?" I asked.

"I'm not sure."

"It's because I didn't get vaccinated, isn't it?"

"You missed getting vaccinated. You were lucky to get the vaccine later, in a sugar cube, remember?"

"I thought that was something like Communion. Then, how did I get polio?"

"No, you don't have polio."

"Then what is it?

"I think it's Guillain-Barré syndrome."

"I've never heard of that. Will he get better?" my mom asked.

"Since he regained some movement the first couple of weeks, he should be normal in a month. A year at the most."

That made me feel a little better. But I was worried because I don't think I've ever been normal.

CHAPTER 13

COWS OUTSIDE

There was probably something simple I could do to get out of the bank, without getting into trouble. I just hadn't thought of it, yet.

After Grandpa had fallen into the basement and almost drowned in the water-soaked trash, my dad tried cleaning out the cellar. It didn't seem possible but there was more trash down there now than before. There was no more room in the cellar. That meant all garbage had to be removed from the house daily and the papers burned in the fire pit. That was my job.

I usually had no problem doing this daily chore compared to everything I had to do each day when we lived on the farm. I had spent so much time finding out what happened to Kenny that I had neglected the only thing I had to do at home. Which meant my dad did it for me. Then I had gotten sick. After I got better, my dad still was doing it. Which meant he reminded me each night that he was doing my work for me.

So, I took the trash out before he got home from work. After he parked his car in its usual spot under the tall oak tree, he got out and stood next to me. I threw the last of the wastepaper into the fire. He looked at me and said with a wink, "Now, that wasn't so hard, was it?"

It reminded me of when we had lived on the farm and one of my chores was to bring the cows in from the pasture for milking each night. The problem was that I dawdled while picking eggs and feeding the chickens. I was always late getting the cows in.

"Do I have to get the cows in myself from now on?" my dad had said. It wasn't just what he said but how he said it. The disappointment in his voice and on his face hurt me more than the beatings some other kids got.

That's when I decided to change the order of things and get the cows in first the next day. It was a hot, muggy summer day. Shep and I walked in the shade of the old oaks and elms on the way to the cows and their normal grazing spot. The pasture was surrounded by hills on all sides, reminding me of the bottom of my cereal bowl. Barbed wire fences separated the cows from our fields of alfalfa, oats, and corn.

When we got there, the cows weren't there. Of course, they would have to pick this day to do this to me.

I cupped my hand over my eyes to shield them from the sun and searched the pasture for any sign of the cows. They were nowhere to be seen. One place they might be was in the gully in the far corner of the pasture.

Shep and I hurried across the pasture, cutting across the swamp instead of following the fence line. That would have taken longer, and I didn't want to be late again. About a quarter of the way through the swamp, I realized that had been a mistake. With each step into the swamp, I had sunk farther down. By the time I was halfway, it was almost up to my knees and each step was harder and harder to make. I could barely pull my leg out to take a step. I looked back and it was just as far to turn around as it was to keep on going. I looked ahead and Shep was already on the other side waiting for me, and she wasn't even muddy. How did she do that?

When I finally made it across, I collapsed in a heap at her feet, exhausted. After resting for a few minutes, I got up, shaking the heavy mud off my legs, and tried to catch up to Shep who was running toward the gully.

The cows weren't there. But what was there was a hole in the fence where our cows had broken through. Shep had already figured out what had happened and was on her way through the fence and into our alfalfa field on the other side. I slowly stepped over the fallen fence, careful not to catch my bare feet on the barbed wire.

From what I could tell there wasn't much for the cows to eat on the other side since we had just cut and baled hay. In fact, our pasture looked much greener. But there our cows were, in the middle of this field, looking lost, standing under an oak tree my dad left there for shade. As I moved closer and closer toward them, I could hear the mooing of a cow. It got louder and louder and not just because I was getting closer. I had heard that sound before and it was usually because a cow was hurt or scared.

Shep was already herding the other cows back toward our pasture when I reached the tree and the source of the commotion. One of the cows, Beulah, had managed to get herself trapped in the tree. The oak was two trees that had grown together, forming a vee about four feet off the ground. Our cow had gotten herself caught in this vee, so her head was on one side and the rest of her on the other. Beulah was straining to pull herself free. The more she pulled, the tighter the hold the tree had on her, and the louder she bellowed. To free herself, all Beulah had to do was move forward and lift her head.

I grabbed her monstrous head and tried to lift but she was intent on doing the opposite and forced her head down toward the ground. Somehow, I had to make her move forward. I called for Shep. I thought if Shep yapped at Beulah's heels, she would move ahead. Instead of moving forward, Beulah swung her rear end back and forth from side to side.

I called Shep off and sat on a nearby alfalfa bale and tried to figure out what to do. Cutting the tree down was an option but even if I could do it, my dad wouldn't like it. And I'd probably injure or kill Beulah in the process.

I could go to get my dad and have him figure out what to do. But there was probably something very simple and obvious I could do. All I had to do was think of it.

While I was sitting there, I looked over at Beulah, wondering why she had done this. Just to make my life more miserable. What had she been doing?

That's when it hit me. I thought of the answer. I was sitting on it. I figured out how Beulah had gotten trapped. She had been on one side of the tree, saw something she wanted to eat on the other side, and stuck her head through to get to it.

I knew what I had to try. I dragged the bale over toward the tree, cut the twine with my pocketknife, and pulled the bale apart.

Beulah calmed down as she watched me bring part of the bale to her. I held it out. Her mouth opened and she chomped into the alfalfa.

Slowly I moved the hay upward. Her head followed along. I moved it higher and higher and toward me and away from the tree. Beulah's head arched upward. I noticed that her neck was no longer jammed into the vee of the tree. I then moved the hay toward her, above her nose near her eyes. At first, she tried to bite into it by turning her head. When that didn't work, she slowly backed under it. As she did this, I kept moving it toward her. Soon her head cleared the crotch of the tree.

I dropped the hay on the other side. It had worked! Beulah, all of her now on one side of the tree, bent down and ate her treat as if nothing had happened.

Shep and I herded Beulah and the rest of the cows into our pasture. I propped one of the fallen fence posts up with another of the posts. The next day, my dad and I would have to mend the fence before the cows could go out to the pasture.

Shep had already started the cows back toward the barn. I ran to catch up to them as they wound their way through the woods on a path they had worn over the years.

Just as we got to the barnyard, I saw my dad approach from the front steps of the house. We had made it just in time for milking. If we had been late, he would have been standing impatiently at the fence waiting for us.

I got the cows into their stalls as my dad moved along in front, closing them inside their stanchions. The last one was Beulah. She was trapped again, this time in her stanchion.

"You got them here on time," my dad said as he moved next to me and rubbed his hand through my hair. "Now, that wasn't so hard, was it?"

CHAPTER 14

WHACK THUNK

My dad would know what to do.

Whack.

Thunk.

Whack.

Thunk.

I was out of rocks. It was time to collect some more. They had to be just the right size. If they were too small or too big, they wouldn't fly as far. They had to be just a little smaller than the ping-pong balls from school and not flat.

I picked up the dented bucket that had too many leaks to be repaired and began another search in the newly plowed field. In just a few minutes, the bucket was filled to the dent in the middle. If I added any more rocks, I wouldn't be able to carry them back to the yard.

I set the bucket near home plate and picked up my bat. Not a baseball bat, but a thin board about the size of the State Fair yardstick only thicker. I had to make new ones every other day because they were always breaking. Home plate was a square of yellow linoleum I had cut from leftover scraps from when Grandpa Joe put a new floor in the kitchen.

I grabbed a rock from the pail and stepped into the batter's box. I was Mickey Mantle, Hank Aaron, and Willie Mays all in one.

I tossed the 'ball' in the air with my left hand while holding the 'bat' with the other. When Whitey Ford released the 'pitch' toward home, I grabbed the 'bat' with both hands and swung.

Whack.

Thunk.

The rock hit the lowest part of the roof of the barn. It was only a single.

A year ago, it would have been a homerun. Grass had already grown over the previous home plates closer to the barn.

"Did you do your chores yet?" my dad yelled from the porch. He was headed to the barn to milk the cows.

"Not yet."

"Well, get 'em done."

"Okay, I will."

If he hadn't been a huge baseball fan, 'I will' wouldn't have been good enough. It would have to be, I'm doing 'em.

"And don't break any windows."

"I won't."

I had learned to place-hit after several close calls. The north end of the barn had no windows, so I became a pull hitter early on.

Anything off the side of the barn was an out, as well as anything that didn't reach the barn.

"Let me try," my older brother, Ron, said. He walked off the porch steps, grabbed the bat from my hands, and stepped to the plate.

'No. You can't."

"I can't? Just watch me."

I paced back and forth.

He tossed a rock in the air and took a wild swing as it came down. Whiff. He wasn't even close. As well as the next five swings. What was I worried about? On the next swing, he hit the rock squarely. It flew in a huge arc, far over the barn and out of sight. Showoff.

The next three as well.

The next one headed in a line toward the side of the barn. The south side. I could see it happen before it did.

Clink.

The window next to the milk house shattered. Ron put the bat in my hands and ran for the house.

"Ow! Jimmie!"

The barn house door flew open. My dad appeared holding his head. Even from home plate, I could see blood running down his face.

As he walked up the hill toward me, I was tempted to turn and run away, but I knew that I would have to face him eventually. I looked toward the house and could see Ron making faces at me through the yellow curtains in the kitchen window.

"Jimmie!"

I turned back to my dad who was almost to my home plate. Hey! Maybe things weren't so bad after all. It wasn't blood! He was wiping his face with his red checkered handkerchief.

"I thought I told you! Is this how you do your chores?"

Maybe things were 'so bad' after all.

"I'll do them right now." I started toward the barn, hoping to avoid a scolding.

"Wait!"

Things were bad. I stopped and walked slowly back to my dad. He was looking at the barn and then at home plate. Back toward the barn. Then at home plate.

"Your home plate is this far back now? You hitting them that far?"

"Most of the time."

"Little boy like you is too small to hit 'em that far."

I wanted to tell him the truth that it was Ron that broke the window. But more than that I wanted my dad to be proud of me and know I could hit the barn from there.

I ran to the pail and picked out a rock, grabbed the bat, and stepped up to the plate.

"Hold it right there, Jimmie!"

My dad looked around the yard, his hands on his hips. He stuck the handkerchief in his back pocket. He bent over home plate and turned it, so it faced away from the barn toward the west. The corn crib, about thirty feet long and fifteen feet high, was about the same distance from home plate.

"Try it."

I stood in the batter's box and tossed the rock in the air. When it came down, I took my hardest swing ever and missed.

"Not so hard. Try again."

This time when the rock came down, I met it squarely with my usual swing. The rock arced toward the corn crib and hit just below the roof. A triple.

"Yep. You sure *can* hit 'em."

I reached for another rock.

"After you do your chores."

"But first…" he continued.

He picked up the bat, looked in the pail for just the right rock. He stepped up to the plate like he had been there before. He took a few practice swings, his overalls riding up his legs showing the white of his legs that hadn't seen the sun for years. The swings were smooth, yet powerful. I had to wonder whether Willie, Mickey, or Hank had as nice a swing as my dad did.

He tossed a rock up and grabbed the bat. The rock jumped off the bat and raced toward the corn crib. I kept waiting for it to slow down but it seemed to rise again when it got over the roof. Soon, it disappeared from my sight making me wonder if it ever did come down.

"Wow!" My mouth was stuck open. My dad looked back at me, a huge grin on his face.

"Dad! I didn't know you could do that."

"I reckon there's a lot you don't know about me. I used to play for the Plum Creek Plums."

"Plums?"

"It wasn't my idea."

He hit a few that went just as far.

Whack. Silence. Whack. Silence. Whack. Silence. Whack. Crack!

My dad stood there with a stunned look on his face. The bat had shattered in his hands.

"I guess I did it that time."

"That's okay. I can make another one."

"No. I'll make you one. A good one."

The next day, I waited after chores for my bat. But my dad hurried out of the barn and into his pickup for a trip to town.

When he got back, I was thinking maybe he had bought one from Busch's store. All he got was udder balm for the cows. The next morning after chores, there was no bat.

After supper that night, I finally had to ask.

"Did you make my bat, yet?"

"Why, sure. I'm surprised you haven't been playing with it already."

"I didn't get the bat."

"I put it by your bed that same night."

Across the table, Ron couldn't contain his laughter.

"Ron, you give Jimmie that bat I made for him."

Ron got up from the table and returned a few minutes later. It was perfect! My dad had even sanded down the handle so it would be easier on my little hands and carved JIMMIE on the bat as well.

My dad went to the closet and dug around for a while until he found what he was looking for.

"I was going to give this to you, Ron. But because of the little trick you pulled, I'm giving this bat to Jimmie."

It was gray and weathered and marks from baseballs that became homeruns covered the end of the bat.

"It's the one I used when I was about your age. Don't be hitting rocks with it, though. Only baseballs. In your first real game."

CHAPTER 15

CORNCRIB CORNCRIB

My first real game came two years later after we moved to town, and I played for the little league team. I should say sat on the bench which I did every game. Our team wore yellow shirts and caps. From where I sat, we looked like ducks running around the field.

In one game we played the orange team. It was the bottom of the ninth and we were behind 3 to 1 with runners on second and third and two outs.

Our star hitter, Marty, was up. He strode confidently to the plate. He just knew he was going to hit a homerun to win the game.

I thought their pitcher was just going to walk him. But the pitch escaped from his little hand and flew straight at Marty's head. He ducked to get out of the way and threw his arms up to protect himself.

Thunk!

The ball hit his bat and then his head. It sounded like it had hit a watermelon. Marty fell to the ground, blood spewing from his nose onto his yellow shirt.

The coach and parents gathered around Marty. A few minutes later he was helped to his feet.

"No way he can bat. Not with his nose bleeding like that."

The coach looked up and down the bench, looking for someone to bat who wasn't me. But I was the only one left.

I grabbed my dad's weathered bat and started for the plate. Some of the other players knew the game was over and that we had lost. I could see it on their faces. Maybe I would be lucky, and the pitcher would hit me in the head, too.

I stepped into the batter's box and eyed the pitcher. I already had one strike against me. The pitcher went into the windup and threw. The ball looked like it was the size of a pea. I swung as hard as I could. I missed it by about a foot. I could hear the groans from our dugout.

That's when I heard my dad shout, "Corncrib! Corncrib!"

I hadn't even known my dad was there! I knew what he was telling me. Just swing nice and easy. Like hitting rocks at the corncrib.

I stood up to the plate and waited for the pitch. This time it looked like a baseball. I took an easy swing and met the ball squarely. In my mind, I saw the ball flying over the centerfield fence. Instead, the bat shattered in my hands. The ball somehow decided to head for the outfield. The shortstop and second basemen and center fielder all tried to make the catch. As I reached first, I saw the ball fall onto the grass for a hit.

One run had already scored. By the time I reached second, the throw from the center fielder flew a foot over the catcher.

I darted for third. I forgot about the pitcher backing up home. I was a dead duck. Why didn't I stay on second?

The third baseman had an easy tag. But he took his eye off the ball. I didn't even slide and rounded the bag as the ball rolled into left field. I forgot about the left fielder. Why didn't I just stay at third?

The catcher was waiting for the throw as I neared home plate. It seemed like it was here to New Market away.

I went into my slide at home plate when I felt it. The ball bonked off my head as I crossed home plate. I was safe.

I had scored the winning run! Not exactly a home run but we had won the game. I was swarmed by my teammates as we jumped up and down, enjoying our win.

I was now part of the team!

After the game, I walked up to my dad.

"Nice hit, Jimmie."

"Sorry I broke your bat."

"That's okay. Bats have only so many hits in them. It's a good thing I saved the last one for you!"

CHAPTER 16

THE MORELS OF THE STORY

The leaves rustled beneath our feet. The sun was shining in the clear blue sky but in the cover of the woods, it seemed like we were walking in moonlight. My dad had gotten me up before dawn. My legs were feeling weak again. I didn't want to say anything to my dad who was walking ahead of me. He would insist that we go home, and we had just gotten there.

We were hunting but without guns or arrows. My dad carried a grocery bag with *Simon's Grocery* in big blue letters on the side as we searched behind trees and under logs.

"What are you two doing here?"

My dad and I looked up to see a lady dressed in red fancy clothes like she was going to church. She looked like Big Red Riding Hood. In her hand, she also held a grocery bag but hers said *Piggly Wiggly* in red letters on the side.

"Hunting here for mushrooms. Just like every year since I can remember," my dad answered.

"Me, too. But it's my first time." She held up her bag. "You probably came for nothing because I think I picked all of them."

My dad looked into the bag. I sneaked a peek in as well.

"Why, you can't eat these. They're toadstools. These are poison," my dad said.

The lady snatched her bag away.

"You're just saying that to get my mushrooms. My mom used to eat these all the time."

"Yes," my dad said. "All the time if it was once. You need to get morels."

"No, I don't! And it's pronounced morals."

"No. You need to pick these." He showed her one from his bag. "This is a morel. Looks sort of like a light brown corn cob."

"Humph. Probably tastes like one, too."

Before my dad could say anything else, she turned and quickly hurried away from us farther into the woods. My dad took a few steps into the woods after her and stopped.

When he came back, he said, "She disappeared. You just can't tell some people anything. Well, let's see if we can fill this bag."

Every morel I found had to pass inspection from my dad before it went into the bag. Sometimes I made a mistake. My dad said my mom didn't know a good mushroom from a bad one, so we had to make sure there were no poison mushrooms in the bag. My mom also said she would never eat mushrooms but more than once I've seen her sampling them when she thought no one was looking.

"How could you miss these? If they had teeth, they would have bit you."

Sure enough, he had found three mushrooms in a spot I thought I had searched thoroughly. It had been happening all day.

"That's okay. You have to develop an eye for them."

My dad sure had one. He could spot them from the pitcher's mound away.

"Help! Help!"

We both turned toward the direction Big Red Riding Hood had gone.

"Now what has she gotten herself into?"

"Help, I said! Help me!"

"We're coming, lady!" my dad yelled.

"Well, hurry then!"

Up ahead, we saw the *Piggly Wiggly* bag on the ground. By the time we finally got to the lady, she had screamed until she was hoarse. Somehow, she had fallen into a deep ravine with no way out. Each time she tried to claw her way out, she would fall back in, rocks and clumps of dirt raining in on top of her.

"Aren't you going to come down here and get me out?"

"If I did that, then there would be two of us stuck down there."

"Well, you aren't just going to leave me here!"

"I am tempted to. But I'll have Jimmie run to the car. I have a rope in the trunk. I think we can get you out with that."

My dad looked at me and I nodded. I ran back toward the car. Very fast at first and then slowing as my legs weakened. Before the sickness, I would have been back already. Then to top it all off, it started to rain. On the way back from the car, I kept slipping and sliding and falling in the mud.

"What took you so long? Did you go to Chicago to get the rope?" my dad joked.

"It seemed more like New York," I answered. I dropped the rope at his feet and collapsed at the base of a huge oak.

"Except you got the wrong rope."

"What?"

"This rope is for men. We need the woman rope."

"What?"

He winked at me.

"Just kidding."

He made a loop at the end of the rope.

"She seems awful quiet."

"I think she yelled herself to sleep. Thank God," he said.

He tossed the loop down to Big Red.

"It's about time!" she screeched. "I'm wet as a dishrag down here."

Together my dad and I pulled Big Red out of the ravine even though I'm sure my dad could have done it alone. A few times he let the rope slip a little causing her to fall back into the ravine. From the smile on his face, I could tell my dad was just having a little fun with her.

When we finally got her out of the ravine, she grabbed her grocery bag and hiked out of the woods without even thanking us.

"Maybe we should have left her there," I said.

"I know. I considered it but…"

We got home just as it got dark. I could tell my mom was worried, but she didn't say anything.

"You got the water boiling?" my dad asked.

"Of course. What else would it be doing with you hunting mushrooms? I always boil them."

My dad gave her a playful hug around her waist.

"Then how about you make us some mushrooms."

My dad and I got cleaned up at the kitchen sink. After my dad lit a cigarette, he went out to the porch to smoke where it was cool. I sat at the kitchen table to keep my mom company. I rested my head in my arms on the kitchen table. I was so tired from the long day I must have fallen asleep almost immediately.

I woke up to the smell of mushrooms frying in the pan. I didn't realize how hungry I was until then.

"Some company you were, sleepyhead. Might as well have been here by myself."

I got up from the table and hugged her around her waist.

"Do something useful like throw that dirty bag away."

She pointed toward the sink and the grocery bag. But it didn't say *Simon's Grocery* on the side. It said *Piggly Wiggly*.

I turned toward my mom who was about to sample a mushroom.

"Stop! Mom! Don't eat them! They're poison."

"I know. That's what I always tell your dad."

"No, they're poison! Dad! Come here quick!"

"What's this?" my dad said as he appeared in the doorway.

"It's the poison bag. See. *Piggly Wiggly*."

"It's okay, Jimmie. She took our bag but it's okay. While you were getting the rope, I emptied her bag and filled it with some good morels I found. Mean as she was, poison mushrooms probably wouldn't hurt her. But I wasn't sure."

CHAPTER 17

THE SORE THUMB

I found a tall desk in the middle of the lobby. It has slips of paper and a pen that is attached to the desk with a chain, apparently so no one would steal it. If you have money to put in the bank, why would you steal a pen?

I played tic-tac-toe for a while. I got bored very quickly. It's no fun playing tic-tac-toe by yourself.

I would rather do anything than sit here and wait for the bank to open. Even deliver newspapers.

Shivering in the cold winter air, I counted out exactly twenty-three newspapers. Each newspaper was getting bigger and heavier. Was it because there was more news now than there was last year when I had first gotten my paper route? I still had the same number of newspapers to deliver to the homes and stores from one end of town to the other.

The cold wind fluttered the newspapers, making it difficult to stuff the last of them into the dirty canvas delivery bag. A headline caught my attention.

CHRISTMAS TREE THIEF ANGERS AREA RESIDENT.

I turned my back to the wind and read the article. Mr. Novotny awoke last Wednesday and discovered one of the fancy pine trees in his front yard had been vandalized. Someone had cut off the top six feet, leaving the bottom three feet looking like a *sore thumb* sticking out of his front yard.

I reread that part. Yes. That was how Mr. Novotny had said it. A sore thumb. He went on to say that if someone had wanted a Christmas tree that bad, all they had to do was ask and he would have given them one from his woods out back.

"Shouldn't you be busy delivering my paper?"

I looked up to see Fritz Tupy, an eighty-year-old retired farmer who lived on the edge of town. He was the second to the last delivery on my route, a mile across town from everyone else.

"No wonder I don't get my paper until it's almost yesterday's."

He turned and spat some Copenhagen into the gutter next to him, getting some on the leg of his overalls. I reached the paper toward him, but he turned it down. I was hoping he would take his paper and save me the trip to his house. He turned and said over his shoulder, "You have that paper waiting for me when I get home, then."

I stuck the paper into the canvas bag and started on my paper route. I started to wonder. Why would you steal a Christmas tree? What was the point? If you had to steal the tree, how could you afford presents to put under the tree? Or did you have to steal those too? Would the thief go to just one house and steal all their presents or just steal one from each house so they wouldn't be missed?

But, again, what was the point? Every time you looked at the tree, wouldn't you feel just the opposite of Christmas?

My first stop was uphill two blocks away to Mr. Jensen's house. I trudged through the snow. The strap of the canvas bag bit into my shoulders from the weight of all the newspapers. The first six deliveries were on the same block making my load six papers lighter. I took the long way around Bull's house to my next stop at the Hennes Feed Mill on the west end of town.

I walked the three extra blocks to avoid Pickle's house just before my last delivery at the Star Café. The smell of fresh bread and the warmth of the restaurant greeted me when I opened the door. Behind the counter, Tillie put her hands on her hips. She frowned.

"About time you brought that paper. It's all old news by the time it gets here."

Every day she would say that. It seemed like everyone on my route said that to me. Then her frown would turn into a smile and then into a huge laugh as if she had made up the funniest original joke ever. Maybe she didn't remember from one day to the next or thought I wouldn't remember.

"What'll it be?" she asked. I slid onto the red fountain stool and looked up at the menu posted on the wall. I don't know why I did that because I knew what I wanted. I pulled off my mittens and blew on my hands to warm them up.

"Looks like you could use some iced tea."

She said that every winter day as well.

"No, thanks. I'll have some hot chocolate, please."

"Suit yourself."

She said that every day as well.

Tillie returned in a few seconds with the steaming cup of hot chocolate. I wrapped my cold fingers around the cup to warm them.

"There. That should warm you up. Ain't you got a warmer coat and better mittens?"

84

"Thanks. I got these a while ago when we were on the farm. These are warm enough though."

"Hmm."

I pushed a nickel toward her to pay for the hot chocolate. She pushed the nickel back toward me.

"Keep it. It's on the house."

She said that every day as well.

I twirled around three times on the red stool and got up to leave.

"What about my paper?"

"Oh. Yeah. Right."

I reached into the canvas bag for the remaining newspaper. That's when I saw it.

"Oh, no!" I whispered.

"Don't tell me you don't have my paper," Tillie accused. She wore that fake frown.

"No. It's just that I have *two* newspapers left! I forgot somebody."

But who? I had made all my deliveries. I was sure of it. Or was I?

"Who did you miss?" Tillie asked.

"I don't know. But I got to find out!"

I slung the canvas bag over my shoulder and darted out the door. I knew what I would have to do. I would have to go over my route again, meaning I might run into Bull or Pickle. At my first three stops, the newspapers still lay where I had deposited them earlier. But at Jim Tremda's house, the paper had been taken inside, if I had even delivered it. To find out I would have to ask. This would be embarrassing.

I made the long, slow steps up his sidewalk. I knocked on his door. I heard the sounds of footsteps making their way to the front door. Jim's round, red face appeared through a crack in the door.

"It's you."

"Yeah. It's me."

"You're not collecting again, are you? I just paid you last week."

"No. I'm not collecting."

"You aren't? Then what is it?"

"Well. Ah. Did you get your paper today?"

A puzzled look appeared on his face.

"What kind of question is that? Did I get my paper?"

He lifted his arm and showed me the paper.

"Of course, I got my newspaper. You delivered it to me so why shouldn't I have it?"

"Okay, thanks." I turned and ran off down his sidewalk.

I took the long way around Bull's house again before the feed mill. Then, I saw there was no newspaper at Mrs. Solek's house. She answered with a smile on her face when she saw me on the doorstep.

"Oh, Jimmie! How nice to see you. Usually, you just drop the paper off and I don't see you. But I already have my paper. See?"

"Oh, good."

"Would you like a kolache?"

I loved those Czech pastries. My mom filled them with apricots, prunes, or poppyseed.

"Do you have any with prunes?"

"Oh, yes. They are my favorite. Most kids don't like them. Be careful I didn't leave a pit inside by mistake."

I had covered my entire route when I figured it out. I had forgotten Fritz Tupy's newspaper. I ran across town to get him his paper. I knew he would be looking out his kitchen window waiting for me. And he was.

On the way home, I detoured and headed toward Mr. Novotny's house. I just had to see that tree.

After I turned the corner by Mary Sheda's house, there it was. I stopped across the street and stared at it. It sure looked out of place in the middle of all the other pine trees.

I held up my thumb next to the topless tree. No. Mr. Novotny was wrong. It didn't look like a sore thumb. It looked more like Howie's head the time he got the flat-top haircut.

"So, you think it's funny!"

I turned to see Mr. Novotny standing next to me.

"No."

"Then why were you laughing?"

Had I laughed out loud? I didn't think I had. I put on my serious face.

"I'm sorry." Then for some reason, I blurted it out. I hadn't even been thinking it. "Could I have a Christmas tree?"

"What?" His face turned a beet red.

"You said if anyone wanted a Christmas tree, all they had to do was ask."

"I know what I said but I didn't mean it."

"You mean you were lying! In the newspaper!"

"No. I just didn't think anyone would take me up on it, is all. I hate losing that tree. I think it was stolen by some kid they call Bull, but I can't prove it."

"Bull?" I asked.

"Yeah, Bull. You know him?"

We just stood there looking at each other and then the tree and then each other and then the ground.

"Yeah, I know Bull. Don't like him though," I finally admitted.

"Come on. Let's go pick you out a tree."

I got home about a half-hour later. The tree I had picked out was about the same size as I was. Most of the needles had fallen off by the time I had dragged it eight blocks home.

Mom was waiting on the porch steps.

"What you got there, Jimmie?"

"I got us a Christmas tree."

"Not another one!"

"Another one. You mean we already got one?"

"Come inside and look."

I followed her through the porch, into the living room. There sat, not one, but three Christmas trees.

"But how?"

"Well, your dad got one, like he usually does. And his boss dropped one by, along with a turkey for Christmas dinner. And your Uncle John brought one by. Since he figured we didn't live on the farm anymore, he cut one out of his woods."

"You know what that means," I said. "This year we each get our own Christmas tree!"

"And you already got a present for your tree."

She showed me a huge box wrapped in red and white Santa Christmas paper. The card on it said, "To Jimmie. From Tillie."

CHAPTER 18

THE SOCK HIT ME

They'll find me in the bank and blame me for something I didn't do.

I had been saving my newspaper money all winter. It's not that I wouldn't have wanted to buy more baseball cards. My collection was still missing Mickey Mantle and Willie Mays. But I did have five Jackie Brandt cards, whoever he was.

As hard as delivering the papers was each day, collecting the money from the customers was even harder. It seemed like no one was ever home when it was time to pay for the paper. The ones that were home almost always said, "Didn't I just pay you last week?"

Or they had a variety of excuses.

Mrs. Thompson would look into her purse and say, "It looks like all I have is this hundred dollar bill. You don't have change for a hundred, do you?" It was probably the same hundred dollar bill each month if there even was one. Just once I would like to have change for that hundred so I could see the look on her face.

Mrs. Petrick would put her hands on her hips and shake her head. "I'm so sorry. My husband has all the money and he's not home from work yet." He must have worked twenty-four hours a day every day of the week because that's where he was, no matter when I stopped by.

And Mr. Pacek had to have used more electricity than anyone in the whole world. His standard answer was, "The electric bill is due this week, can I pay you next week? Can't expect a man to live without electricity, can you?" Well, yes, I thought. My Uncle John did.

It amazed me how Mr. Pacek, who demanded his paper be delivered promptly at five o'clock each day, had no problem paying me late each month.

The most unusual excuse happened at Mrs. Hudanek's house. She usually paid me promptly each month. That's why it surprised me when she said she didn't have the money. What surprised me, even more, was when she said, "Little Tomas ate your money." Little Tomas wasn't so little. I looked at the plump little boy wallowing in the corner and it seemed like he had been eating a lot more than money. Like anything that got near him.

I was starting to feel nervous being in the same room with him.

Didn't little Tomas know I was saving for a new bicycle, just like the one I didn't win from Axel? Each cent I made I hid in a sock that I kept in the back of the top shelf of my closet.

Howie, my new friend from town, already had a bike like the one I wanted. He said when I got my new bicycle, we'd ride all around town together. He seemed just as excited by this as I was. Each day he would ask me how much I had hidden in that sock and if I had enough for the new, blue Schwinn.

Mrs. Devrek always had the newspaper money. But she had a dog outside. A big dog. A big dog that would bark and snarl and was held back by a thin rope attached to a flimsy nail that was about to come out of the wall.

Just as I was about to give up and run away, Mrs. Devrek would open the door. The dog would magically turn itself into a cuddly puppy dog. "Don't worry. Little Poo Bear here wouldn't hurt a fly. Besides, his bark is worse than his bite."

How did she know that? How many paperboys has the dog bitten? And did she ask the paperboys which was worse - the bark or the bite?

I had just finished collecting one April evening and stopped at the Star Café. *The Wanderer* was playing on the jukebox. The high school girls in bobby sox and billowing skirts flirted with the teenage boys in white T-shirts with cigarette packs rolled up in the sleeves.

Howie was at the counter surrounded by almost every kid from our class. He saw me come in and smiled broadly and waved me over.

"Come on. Have a malt on me."

"Yeah," Teddy said. "He's treating everyone."

By the time I got through the crowd of kids to the counter, Tillie had a strawberry malt waiting for me.

"Thanks, Howie," I said.

"Don't mention it, Jimmie. We're friends, right?"

Before I could answer, Marty got in between us.

"Can I have another malt, Howie?"

"Sure. Have two more if you want."

"That sure is a nice new coat you have there, Howie," Marty said.

"Yeah. It's genuine leather."

I dug into my malt and thought how much more fun it was being a town kid. If I was on the farm now, I would probably be cleaning out gutters or slopping the hogs.

I got home about an hour later. Tired from delivering papers and collecting. Overjoyed from spending a fun time with my new friends. But so full from the three malts, there was no way I could eat supper.

I just wanted to run upstairs to my room to add my money to my sock. And be that much closer to my new bike.

I opened the door to my closet. Books rained down upon me along with my baseball glove and other toys I had stacked neatly on the top shelf.

At the same time, I heard my mom yell from downstairs.

"Howie stopped by when you were gone." I found the sock on the floor.

The sock was empty.

CHAPTER 19

THE WHITE HOUSE

The next day we walked the few blocks to Howie Tronski's house. We being my mom, my dad, Grandpa Joe, Uncle John, Uncle Vencil, and Aunt Mara. I had told my mom about the money missing from my sock, who told my dad who told Uncle John who told Uncle Vencil who told Aunt Mara. No one told my Grandpa Joe, but he came along even though he didn't know why.

My dad rang the doorbell of Howie's house, which looked like Scarlet's house in *Gone with the Wind*. Howie's mother answered the door. She seemed quite surprised to find us all on her doorstep. For one thing, we had her outnumbered.

She looked like a movie star with her hair in a fancy perm. She wore makeup and jewelry and a purple dress covered with a clean, frilly white apron.

"I'm sorry I'm such a mess. I've been busy cleaning all morning."

I had to wonder what she looked like when she wasn't a mess.

At first, it looked like she wanted to shut the door on all of us. Instead, she opened the door wide.

"Where are my manners? Please come on in."

My parents made no move to enter the house. None of us did. I could only stare at the whitest, cleanest living room with the whitest, cleanest carpet I had ever seen. Did anyone walk on that carpet? From the looks on my parent's faces, I knew what they were thinking. There was no way we could go in that house. Our shoes were caked with mud from walking across our muddy yard.

"We'll just stand out here, if that's fine with you," my mom finally said.

"You must be Jimmie's family. What can I do for you? Is everyone all right?"

"Why, yes, we're all fine. But I think there is something wrong."

"Damn right there's something wrong!" Uncle John yelled.

"You be quiet," my dad said. "You said you wouldn't say anything if we let you come along."

Howie's mom looked worried and confused, wringing her hands in her apron.

"My dear sakes, what is it?"

"You tell her, Jimmie," my mom said to me.

Me? It wasn't my idea to come over here. I had wanted to forget about the whole thing. I tried to talk but there was nothing in my mind so there was nothing to come out.

"Go ahead, Jimmie. Tell her."

Still more nothing.

Finally, Aunt Mara spoke up.

"It's the money, Mrs. Tronski."

"Money? What money?"

"Little Jimmie's newspaper money."

Now Howie's mom was more confused.

"Are you all here to collect for the newspaper? But we just paid last Saturday. I'm sure of it. And Jimmie's not our paperboy."

"No, it's not that. You tell her, Jimmie."

After what seemed like a minute of everyone looking at me, I finally spoke.

"My sock is empty."

If she wasn't confused before, she really was now. She stared down at my feet. It was her turn not to have anything to say.

Finally, Aunt Mara came through again.

"It seems that all Jimmie's newspaper money is missing. He kept it in a sock in his closet. When he came home last night, the sock was empty."

"I'm so sorry to hear that."

She actually did look sorry, too.

"The trouble is, Mrs. Tronski," Aunt Mara continued, "is that your son, Howie, was in Jimmie's room alone."

"And you think that Howie? No. That can't be. There must be some mistake."

"I told you it wouldn't do any good," Uncle John bellowed.

"Shut up, John," my dad said, for all the good it would do.

"Howie has his own money. Why would he steal from you?"

"Tell her the rest, Jimmie."

Tell her the rest? I hadn't even wanted to tell her the beginning.

"He was buying everyone stuff at the Star Café yesterday."

I could see a smile like my mom's on Howie's mom's face.

"How nice! Howie always is so generous with his money."

"You mean Jimmie's money!" My Uncle John interrupted. "I knew she would stick up for him."

"Shut up, John!" Mara said.

There was a long pause where no one had anything to say to anyone. My mom looked at Mara. Mara looked at Vencil. Vencil looked at John. John looked at me. My dad just looked down at the front steps like he didn't want to be there. I didn't either.

Finally, Howie's mom turned and got her purse from the kitchen.

"I'm sorry, Jimmie. How much did you say you were missing?"

She opened her purse and took out her billfold.

"Let me see how much I have in here."

"No, wait," my dad said. "We don't want any money. We just want to talk to Howie. Find out what happened."

"Like I said. Howie's not here."

"Then would you please ask him when he comes home? Find out for us?"

Her warm smile reappeared.

"I will do that, Sir. I surely will."

She called my dad 'sir!'

Then everyone stood there for a few seconds just smiling and nodding at each other until my folks turned to leave.

After Howie's mom closed the door, Uncle John spoke up.

"We should have got the money when we had the chance. Now we'll never get it back."

"Shut up, John!" everyone said. Everyone except me.

"What money?" Grandpa Joe asked.

At first, I didn't think going to see Howie about my money was a good idea. Now I was sure it wasn't.

When we got back to our house, my mom sent me up to straighten my room. I gathered up everything that had fallen from the shelf in my closet. Monopoly pieces and game dice littered the floor. I reached up to put my baseball glove on the top shelf.

Then the sock hit me.

It was no longer empty. Had I imagined it being empty last night? Did I cause all this trouble for nothing?

"I hope you don't mind."

I jumped about a foot in the air from fright. When I turned around, I saw my brother, Ron, lying on my bed. He didn't even live here anymore.

"If you mean your dirty shoes on my pillow, yes I mind."

"No. That I had to borrow your newspaper money last night."

"You mean you stole my money?"

"No. I borrowed it."

"Without telling me?"

"So what? I paid you back."

His face turned red with anger. He stomped from the bed to my closet, pushing me to one side. He picked the sock up from the floor and dumped its insides onto the floor. Quarters, nickels, and dimes splattered against the hard wood and hid in my dirty clothes.

"See. It's all there. Every last cent."

"It's too late now. You should have told me."

I sat down on the floor and began to scoop coins back into the sock. I looked up at Ron and the puzzled look on his face. He knelt on the floor next to me.

"It was just one day. I didn't think you'd miss it."

"We thought Howie took it. Everyone went to get it back from Howie. At his house. From his mom!"

"Everybody?"

I nodded my head.

He shook two dimes and a quarter out of a pair of my dirty underwear.

"Howie's here for you!" My mom's voice carried up the stairs.

"You should have told me." I slowly got up as my brother continued to pick money off the floor. "You should have told me."

Howie was waiting outside for me, pacing back and forth. When he saw me come out of the porch, he glared at me. He turned away, picked up a rock, and threw it at a power line pole, missing it completely.

"My mom! How come you had to go to my mom?" He said all this without turning around to look at me. He picked up another stone and threw it at the pole, missing it again.

"I didn't know. I mean. My mom said you…"

"Why not just ask me?" he asked as he turned toward me. "I thought you were my friend."

"You ARE my friend! I'm sorry." Tears streamed down my cheeks. "You ARE!"

"No. I WAS!"

He picked up another stone and threw it at the pole. This time it hit with a loud thunk that echoed through our yard.

"You WERE my friend!" he shouted and ran out of our yard.

My mom told me Howie would get over it. That he would forget about the whole thing after Ron went over and apologized to Howie's mom. That was Ron's punishment. It would all be forgotten. I knew better.

CHAPTER 20

ELMER AND DARLA

I looked up at a clock above the entrance to the bank. It is 3:11. The middle of the night. It felt like I've been trapped in here for days.

I was sure I am going to be arrested. The thought of being locked up or sent to a reform school didn't appeal to me. Maybe I could run away and join the carnival.

A carnival was coming to New Prague. I had never been to a carnival before but according to Uncle John, it was more fun than threshing. That was saying something. Threshing was his favorite time of the year.

He owned and operated the threshing machine that he would move from farm to farm to harvest oats. Farmers would take turns helping each other out. I would go on rides on wagons or tractors. There were big meals and desserts and every kind of pop I could ever want.

If a carnival was more fun than that, I wanted to go. I was now almost recovered from the mysterious illness with the name I couldn't remember. My mom wasn't sure it was a good idea.

"He'll be too weak," my mom said. "What if he gets a relapse? It'll be too much walking, too much excitement."

"It'll be good for him," my dad answered.

So, I got to go. The only thing was, Ron had to watch and make sure I was okay every second.

When we got there, Ron and I sort of agreed to go our separate ways so we could both have fun. He gave me one whole dollar and he disappeared into the crowd.

I didn't know there were this many people in all of New Prague. All of them were taller than I was. I threaded my way through the legs, listening to the cheerful music from the rides and smelling hot dogs, hamburgers, and French fries from the food stands.

The crowd cleared in front of the cotton candy booth. I had never heard of cotton candy. I wondered if I should get something if I didn't know what it was. And it cost five whole cents.

A lady with perspiration under her arms and running down her face, stuck a paper cone into a glass case. Magically the cone was covered with pink fuzz. As she twirled the cone around and around, it grew into a giant pink cotton ball. I had to have one. Even if it was five whole cents.

It tasted sweet as it disappeared in my mouth with each bite. I guess I didn't know how to eat one of these things because my face and hands were so sticky that if I bumped into someone, I would probably end up stuck to him forever.

Behind one of the booths, I saw a hose. That was just what I needed. When I squeezed back there, a dark-skinned boy dressed in a torn shirt and pants was on the other end of the hose. He was running back and forth washing kettles and pots and sweating as much as the lady in the booth.

I edged closer to him and held my hands out toward the stream of water. It took him a few seconds but then he splashed some water on my hands so I could un-sticky my hands and face.

"Cotton candy?" he asked.

I nodded yes.

"What's the matter? Can't you talk?"

"I've been sick," I answered.

"With what?"

"I can't say it."

He looked puzzled.

"It must have been bad if you can't talk about it."

"I mean, I can't remember the name of it and if I did, I couldn't pronounce it."

"That's even worse. What's your name?"

"Jimmie."

He came over to me and offered his hand. Even with knowing I'd had something I couldn't pronounce, he wasn't afraid to shake my hand.

"I'm Pepe."

Peppy. That was an appropriate name for him.

"We can talk while I work. Being a town kid, you wouldn't know about chores."

I guess I didn't look like a farm kid anymore.

"I used to be a farm boy. We had a farm just outside of town and moved here about two years ago."

"Same town. All your life. That must be nice. I'm always someplace different."

My legs were starting to get weak underneath me and I needed to sit down. That had never happened to me before. I hoped it wasn't my sickness coming back. I sat down on one of many boxes of sugar and food coloring behind the booth. Pepe found a few more kettles to clean.

"Isn't it fun to travel all over and see new places?" I asked.

"Not if you're working all the time."

"What about the rides? You must get to go on them."

"If I have the time, yes."

The cotton candy lady stuck her head behind the booth and shouted something at Pepe. I couldn't understand it since it wasn't English or Czech.

"Si. Si. Mamacita."

He dropped the hose and turned off the water.

"Jimmie, you have to get up. Mama wants these boxes inside."

"I'll help you with the boxes. And with your other chores. Then your mama might let you go on some rides with me."

Pepe smiled.

Working together, the time flew by. Pepe said we finished everything in a third of the time it would have taken if he had done them by himself. That didn't make sense to me. With two of us, it should have taken half the time.

We squeezed our way out into the crowd which had gotten larger. Who were all these people and where did they come from?

"Let's go on this ride," I said to Pepe.

"The Merry-go-round?"

It looked like fun to me.

"Didn't you ride real horses on your farm?"

"Yes. Those were work horses. These look like fun."

"These just go round and round. They're for little kids."

He was right. There were just little kids going around and around and up and down. But I had never been on one before and it did look like fun.

Next, we came to the Tilt-A-Whirl.

"Now this one we should go on," Pepe said.

I looked at the spinning seats and knew I couldn't go on that ride. I saw other kids on the Tilt-A-Whirl, but they weren't laughing. They were screaming. Why would I want to go on a ride that made me scream? The truth was, I was too afraid. I couldn't admit that to Pepe.

"Let's go on that one instead," I said, pointing to the Ferris wheel.

We rushed toward the giant, lighted spinning wheel. Only four kids were waiting in line, but that was four kids too many for me. I started running so that nobody else got in line ahead of us, dragging Pepe along behind me.

That's when I saw Howie and about four other town kids, also heading for the Ferris wheel. I hadn't seen or talked to him since I had blamed him for something he hadn't done. He would be right behind us in line. I would have to talk to him. What would I say to him? What would he say to me?

As much as I wanted to see our house from the top of the Ferris wheel, perhaps even see our old farm and maybe even see the Foshay Tower in Minneapolis, I stopped and pulled Pepe aside. We hid behind a popcorn stand and watched as Howie and the others got on the Ferris wheel.

"Let's go this way," I said to Pepe.

"But I thought you wanted to go on that ride."

"I did. But now I'm afraid." Which wasn't a lie.

"I get to go on more rides by myself than when you're with me," Pepe said.

"Let's see if I can win a prize for my mom." I pointed toward a ring toss booth. "Let's try that one."

"Nobody ever wins at that," Pepe said.

Next, we came to a booth with three rifles where people were shooting at little yellow ducks that moved across the back curtain.

"How about this one?"

"Nobody ever wins at that," Pepe said.

"This one then?" I said pointing to a basketball free-throw shooting booth.

"Nobody ever wins at that," Pepe said.

He was probably right. The basketballs did look too big to fit through the hoops. We passed four other booths where nobody ever won anything and came to a booth where you threw baseballs at three milk bottles stacked in a pyramid. All you had to do was knock them all off the stand in one toss. There was a giant stuffed bear on the top shelf I knew my mom would like.

"This is the one," I said.

"But nobody…"

"I know but I'm going to try it anyhow."

When I was on the farm, I not only hit homeruns over the corncrib, but I also threw baseballs at a square I had marked on the side of the barn. I would have pretend games where I was a major league pitcher like Warren Spahn or Whitey Ford.

I paid my five cents and was handed a soft and worn grey baseball. I aimed, went into my windup, and pitched toward the bottles. The ball flew up and to the right, almost hitting the stuffed bear on the top shelf. With that one, I wouldn't have hit the broad side of a barn.

"I told you so," Pepe laughed.

"One more try."

I reached into my pocket for another nickel. This time the ball was less worn and a little harder. Again, I aimed, went into my windup, and threw. This time the ball headed straight for the target and hit directly between the bottom two bottles. Magically the bottles flew completely off the stand.

"You did it!" Pepe yelled.

"I was just lucky I guess."

Jumping up and down, I pointed to the top shelf and screamed, "I want that bear! I want that bear!"

The man behind the booth reached up and grabbed something off the bottom shelf and handed it to me.

"All you get is this trinket."

I didn't know what a trinket was, but it sure didn't look like anything my mom would want.

"Every time you win," Pepe said, "you can trade in your prize and move up one shelf."

I looked at all the shelves and there were more shelves than all the nickels and luck I had on me. As I turned to leave, I saw Pepe whisper something to the man behind the booth.

"Wait, son. I made a mistake. You really should have won this here kewpie doll."

I handed his trinket back and examined the kewpie doll. It wasn't as good as the giant stuffed bear, but it was something my mom would like.

"I guess I'm luckier than I thought."

"Yes," Pepe said. "He usually doesn't make mistakes."

Over Pepe's left shoulder, I saw Howie and the others making their way through the crowd. I grabbed Pepe's hand and dragged him behind the booth.

"What's the matter, Jimmie?"

"Howie's out there. I'm kind of avoiding him."

Pepe put his chin in his hand and thought for a few seconds.

"I know. We can see Elmer and Darla."

This time he dragged me around the trailers and pickup trucks. My legs were getting weak again and I didn't know how much farther I could go. We stopped at a trailer painted with stars and moons and comets. He knocked on the door and a man's voice said we could come right in.

The interior of the trailer was also decorated with stars and moons and comets. In the dim light, I could see that all the furniture was my size, making the tiny trailer seem twice as big.

"Elmer. This is Jimmie."

Elmer was also my size, but he looked the same age as my dad. He sat at a small table, a bottle of whiskey in front of him and a cigar that he could barely wrap his fingers around in his mouth. He sort of looked like Elmer Fudd from one of the comics that I read.

"What's the matter? Never see a midget before?"

"No. What's a midget?"

"A small person."

"How come you stopped growing? Was it smoking? Mom always said smoking would stunt my growth."

Elmer let out a huge laugh. "That's a good one, Jimmie."

He took a drink from the whiskey bottle and took a puff from his cigar.

"No, this is as big as I would ever get. And a good thing too. Or else I never would have met Darla. Plus, it helps me in my job as a handyman here at the carnival."

He held his little hands in front of him.

"I can get these in places to fix things here no one else can get to."

Uncle John could use him. He was always complaining about them making machines so he couldn't get his hands in to fix them.

The trailer door opened, and a woman midget dressed in a long, flowing gown entered. Elmer introduced me to Darla. She was a beautiful lady with long black hair and dark eyes that seemed a little too big for her face. She sat next to Elmer and stared at me with those huge eyes.

For what seemed like hours, Elmer told us stories of his travels with the carnival. Pepe and I just listened. Darla intently stared at me.

Darla, who had not spoken a word the whole time, said, "It is time for you two to go."

"Darla is right. It is late," Elmer agreed.

"But first, Pepe's friend, you must know these things," Darla said. "Winning the doll wasn't just luck. You must apologize to your friend in town again. And your legs will get better."

When we got outside, my legs were shaking.

"How did Darla know?"

"She just knows things," Pepe said.

The carnival grounds were empty. I said goodbye to Pepe. I knew I probably would never see him again. And I knew I would have to apologize to Howie.

CHAPTER 21

SORRY ISN'T ENOUGH

I wanted the walk to Howie's house to take longer with each step. I knew when I got there, I would come face to face with Howie and finally have to apologize. Would he just slam the door in my face? I wouldn't blame him if he did.

I squinted into the bright sunlight as I walked to the front door of Howie's house. The grass was freshly cut, and the flowers were neatly arranged around the exterior of the house. At our house, weeds and shrubs were free to take over any part of the yard they wanted.

Howie's mom answered the door. Again, she was dressed in a fancy white, perfectly fitting dress. Her hair was perfectly set, not a hair out of place.

"Is Howie home?"

"Howie's not here now, Jimmie. But he should be home shortly. Would you like to come in?"

I carefully stepped inside the door onto a rug that looked like no one had ever set foot on it. Did she buy a new one for each day? I stood there unable to move as she elegantly moved to the couch and gracefully sat down.

"Please come on in," she said, patting her hand on the couch next to her. "Sit down. Make yourself at home."

Make myself at home? That wasn't going to happen.

I crept toward the couch. I figured the slower I walked, not as much dirt would get on her carpet. I wished that her couch was covered with plastic like my Aunt Thelma used. I was afraid the dirt and smells from our house would end up on her couch.

"Jimmie, I heard you were quite ill. You seemed to have recovered very nicely."

"Yes, pretty much."

"We were all so worried about you."

"You were?"

"Why yes, as a matter of fact, we were."

She sat up straight, shaking her head. What did I do? I looked down to see what I had done to her couch.

"Oh my! Where are my manners? I haven't offered you any refreshments. Are you hungry?"

"No, thank you."

"Let me fix you a sandwich and some milk."

She got up and hurried off to the kitchen. In the thick carpet, the marks from her high heels followed behind her. Looking around the room, I could see everything was perfectly arranged. There was a place for everything, and everything was in its place. In our house, everything was where it wanted to be, which was where the last person had left it.

Howie's mom called me into the kitchen and sat me at the table. In another room, there was another fancier table with eight chairs, three on each side and one at each end. What did they need two tables for?

She placed the sandwich and milk in front of me.

"It's a peanut butter and banana sandwich. I hope you like it."

The idea of peanut butter and bananas in a sandwich seemed as strange to me as if it had been sauerkraut and ice cream. Maybe it was all she had left for a sandwich. She would probably think of the lard and sugar sandwiches my mom made for us as strange. Howie's mom had cut all the crust from the bread. I know my mom and dad would think that was just wasting food.

I tentatively took a bite, expecting the worst.

"This is good!"

"It's Howie's favorite."

Sometimes new things aren't so bad, I thought. I finished the sandwich as fast as I could and then washed the peanut butter from the roof of my mouth with milk.

"I'd better go."

"No, wait. Howie should be here soon. Why don't you watch some television?"

She turned it on. But the screen didn't turn from black to black and white. It turned into a color picture. I wondered what my mom and dad would think of this. Uncle John wouldn't believe it. He still didn't believe in black and white television even though he had seen it.

I didn't pay attention to what I was watching. The colors made everything look so real. Like the people could walk out of the television into the living room.

"Howie's home!"

I turned to see Howie, but he wasn't alone. At his side stood Lawrence, a tall, skinny, red-haired kid whose dad owned half of the town. The half that was worth owning according to Lawrence.

"What's he want?" Lawrence said. His look made me feel like I didn't belong there. Maybe I didn't.

"I better go," I said.

"No, Jimmie can stay, Lawrence. Didn't you have something to say to Howie, Jimmie?" his mom asked.

"Yes, but… I don't know."

"I can take a hint. I'll leave you boys alone."

After she left the room, I wondered why Lawrence couldn't take a hint, too.

Howie finally spoke up. "What did you have to say to me?"

"Not with him here."

"I'm not leaving because of you," Lawrence said. "I'm a guest here. Howie invited me, right?"

Howie looked like he didn't know what to do, like he was in the middle of a hot box with no way out.

"You can say it in front of Lawrence. Go ahead."

"I just wanted to say how sorry I was. It was wrong of me to treat you like that. I know you can't ever forgive me…"

"Your darn right he can't. What? Did your mom and dad make you come over here?"

"Let him finish, Lawrence."

"No. He's sorry. But it's the wrong kind of sorry. The one where you don't mean it."

"No. I mean it."

"Yeah, right. Like the kids in one of my dad's stores that get caught stealing and then apologize only because they have to."

"No," I said, tears rolling down my cheeks. "My folks didn't make me. I am sorry. I really am."

Howie didn't answer but just looked back and forth at Lawrence and me.

I turned and ran out of the house, expecting and hoping that Howie would tell me to stop, that everything was okay. But all I heard was silence. When I reached the street, I just knew Howie and Lawrence were back there laughing at me.

By the time I reached home, I couldn't cry anymore. I sat on our front steps, trembling.

I did notice that my legs weren't tired.

CHAPTER 22

SNOW FOR CHRISTMAS

Or I could run away to Florida.

My newspaper route took me past the blonde girl's house. I didn't know anything about her because her family had just moved to town. She was about my age and cute. There was just something about her.

Each day I hoped I would see her as I rode by. If she happened to be sitting on her porch or playing in her front yard, I would slow down and walk my bicycle down the street. Sometimes she would wave to me.

One day as I neared her house, I saw her sitting on the curb by the driveway. She smiled when she saw me and stood up. I stopped next to her.

"Daddy says he wants your paper."

She had blue eyes.

"Uh, sure. Okay."

I looked at her neighbor's vegetable garden like I had never seen one before. She was too pretty to look at.

"Daddy wants to know if you can start tomorrow."

"Uh. Here. How about today? I got an extra," I said, even though I didn't.

When she took it, I saw her fingernails. They were colored a strawberry red.

"Thank you, so much."

"You're welcome." I couldn't think of anything else to say. I wondered if her fingernails tasted liked strawberries.

"I better go."

I jumped on my bike and headed toward Fritz Tupy's house.

"My name is Violet!"

I turned to her.

"Mine's Jimmie!"

I turned back just in time to run into a parked car. I looked back to see if Violet had noticed. Thank goodness she had already gone into her house.

Each day she would run out to the street to get a newspaper as I rode by. We would just look and smile at each other, not saying anything. Then she would turn and run to the house.

One day, she did have something to say.

"Jimmie, I'm having a birthday party on Saturday. Can you come? Please? I don't know many kids here. So, can you?"

"Uh. Sure. Thanks."

I was glad she didn't know many kids.

"Three o'clock!" She turned and ran to her house. "And we're having pony rides! I bet you've never ridden a horse before."

I was glad she didn't know I was raised on a farm. If she had known, maybe she wouldn't have invited me.

"A birthday party!" my mom said. "What are you going to wear to a birthday party?"

"What about what I got on?"

She looked at my torn shirt and patched blue jeans and shook her head.

"No. You can't wear that. And everything else you have is just the same. And we can't afford…"

She put her head in her hands and thought. When she looked up, her face had brightened.

"I know. You can wear your Cousin Bob's suit."

What was she thinking? Bob was ten years older than me and almost as big as my dad!

"But Mom! Won't it be too big?"

"No, Bob used to be about your size. And I'm sure your Aunt Rose still has it. She never throws anything away."

Pretty soon Aunt Rose was going to run out of clothes for me in her closet.

"And we have to get Violet a present, too."

"What do you get for a present for a girl? What if she doesn't like what I bought for her?"

"I'll think of something," my mom said. "It'll be fun to buy something for a girl for a change."

On Friday, she went to the Kuzelka's Variety store to buy the present. She returned with a birthday gift that was already wrapped in pink flowery paper with a yellow ribbon and bow. I was afraid to ask what was inside.

On the way back, she had stopped to pick up Bob's suit. It looked like it had just come from Simon's store. Maybe Bob only wore it to church for a wedding or funeral.

"Try this on," Mom said. She held the dark blue coat open for me to slip my arms into the sleeves. I had just been out playing in the yard and hoped that the sweat wouldn't ruin the coat and take all the new out of it.

"Turn around," she said as she took a step back.

"It fits perfect! You're built just like your cousin."

Did that mean I would look like him in ten years? I hoped so.

That night, my mom put the suit in the closet. Aunt Rose also had given me a pair of shoes that were a little big, a white shirt that was a little too small, and a black bow tie that snapped onto the collar. I was all set for the party.

I had trouble falling asleep that night. There were a lot of parties at the farm where all the relatives and neighbors would attend. I was sure the birthday party wouldn't be anything like any of those. There wouldn't be any accordion music or beer.

There were probably things that town kids did or didn't do at these parties I didn't know about. Was it okay to eat with your hands? My mom said no but a sandwich or cookie you have to eat with your hands.

Saturday morning, my dad got me up early and took me out to Uncle John's farm to help with the baling. By noon, it seemed like we had just started. At two o'clock, we were still hard at work, and it looked like we were going to stay until we were done.

Finally, I had to tell him.

"I need to get back for the party."

"Party. What party?"

"The birthday party. For Violet. At three."

"Today! I forgot. I can't see as how we can leave yet."

"But Dad…"

"Okay. Let's go. I'm taking you home."

It took forever and by the time we got there, it was almost three o'clock. I still had to wash the baling off and get dressed. I was going to be late for my first birthday party.

"You're late!" my mom said, in case I didn't already know it. She had already filled the tub with water.

"Get those clothes off and get cleaned up. I'll get your suit from the closet."

I left a trail of clothes from the front door and splashed into the bathwater which had turned cold.

"Oh, no!" I heard my mom scream from the other room.

I quickly got out of the tub and dried off on my way to the bedroom. My mom was sitting on the bed, in tears, holding the suit coat in her hands.

"A mouse got to it. Look."

She held the coat up toward me, showing me where a flap over one of the pockets had been chewed.

Of all the clothes in that closet, why had the mouse chosen the suit? There were clothes on hangers and rags and dirty laundry on the floor. I checked the pocket to see if there was cheese or crackers inside where mice would want to get to it.

"I can't mend this," she said. She thought a little while longer. "I know. You can tuck the flap inside the pocket. Like this. See, you can hardly tell."

"Unless you were looking at it," I said.

"You want to go to that party, don't you?"

I nodded yes.

"Then get dressed."

By the time I got to the party, everyone else had arrived. Violet said she didn't know many kids in town, but there were a lot of kids at her party. I had hoped to sneak in without anyone noticing. Instead, they stopped playing some game where Marty was blindfolded and had a horse's tail in his hand. Everyone stared at me as I entered.

I would never be late for anything ever again.

My plan was to keep my right arm over the chewed flap. Doing things with only my left hand was going to be difficult but I would have to figure out a way to do it.

Luckily, they went back to the game as Violet ran up to me. She wore a frilly pink dress, pink shoes, and white anklets.

"I was afraid you weren't coming."

"Sorry."

"I'm just glad you're here."

A man about the size of my dad joined us. He was dressed in the fanciest suit I had ever seen.

"And who is this, Violet?"

"This is Jimmie."

"I've heard a lot about you, young man."

Then it happened. He held out his right hand for me to shake. I didn't know what to do. If I lifted my right arm, Violet would surely see the flap. Maybe I could use my left hand, claiming that I had injured my other arm.

Slowly I lifted my right arm to shake his hand. I looked down to see if the flap was showing. Which caused both Violet and her dad to look down to see what I was looking at. Of course, the damaged flap was sticking out for them to see. I turned in embarrassment to run from the party.

"Wait! Jimmie, don't go," Violet said.

I turned back.

"Daddy, don't you think it's too warm in here for the boys to be wearing those coats?"

"Why, I think you're right."

He took off his own suit coat and went around the room taking the coats from the boys.

Violet helped me get out of mine.

"Isn't that better?"

"Yeah. Thanks."

Except now everyone could see that my shirt was too small.

Whenever I would stop by with the newspaper, she would be waiting or would run out to meet me.

Little by little I found out more and more about her. Her family moved a lot. She said she had lived in four different towns in Minnesota.

What did her dad do that they had to move around so much? She didn't know but with a house like they had, whatever it was had to pay a lot of money. And in our small town, what could that be?

It was nearing the end of summer and school was about to begin. I found out she was going to attend St. Wenceslaus School and would be in Sister Florida's class with me.

One day when I turned the corner by her house, I saw a huge moving van parked in her driveway. Men in gray coveralls were carrying furniture and boxes out of the house and packing it inside the truck.

Violet was sitting on the curb, waiting for me.

"I guess we won't be needing the paper anymore," she said. She looked like she had been crying. "Unless you can deliver it to Florida."

"To Sister Florida?"

"No, the state of Florida. I have to move again. It always happens. Just when I get to know somebody and make some friends, we have to move."

She looked toward the van and watched as they moved a white dresser inside. How could they fit everything from that big house into that little truck? When she turned back to me, I could see a tear run down her cheek.

"Florida is a long way away," she said.

"I could write to you."

"Would you?"

"For sure."

Later that day, I watched from Fritz Tupy's house a block away. The moving van slowly pulled out of the driveway. I watched as Violet walked from the house and into a green and white Ford station wagon.

We had already said goodbye. She didn't know her new address in Florida, so I gave her mine. She said she would write to me the very first thing she did when she got there.

Then I thought of one more thing I wanted to tell her. I jumped on my bike and pedaled as fast as I could. I dropped the newspaper bag to lighten my load. I had to, I needed to talk to her before she left town. I wanted to tell her I'd miss her.

Their car was behind the moving van which was going slow enough for me to catch up to them. I was half a block away when the worst thing happened. The station wagon passed the moving van and turned left out of town. I stopped and sat on the curb at the edge of town. She was gone.

Each day I checked the mailbox for her letter. Each day it wasn't there. That was to be expected. Florida was a long way from Minnesota. If it took a day for a letter to get from New Market to New Prague, it would probably take weeks for it to make its way from Florida.

After a month, I stopped waiting.

But I didn't stop wondering. Even as my dad and I were playing catch in the front yard. Why didn't she write to me like she had said? Had I said something wrong? I wish I had caught up with them that last day and told her what I wanted to tell her.

"Is something wrong, Jimmie?"

My dad was standing next to me. He put his huge hand on my shoulder.

"No, why?"

"Well, you've been dropping every other ball I throw to you. And now you didn't even see the one that flew right past your ear."

"I'll go get it."

I turned to fetch the ball that had rolled into Mrs. Bilek's yard.

"No. Wait, Jimmie. Where's your mind at?"

Should I tell him? Would he understand? He'd think I was stupid. There was no way I could tell him.

"It's Violet." Somehow, I blurted it out. "She said she'd write, and she didn't. And I can't write to her because I don't know her address. That's all. Let's just forget it."

My dad sat down on the front steps and patted his hand on the cement for me to sit down.

"Let's see what we can figure out here." I sat on the edge of the step, looking up at him. "I think you should write to her."

"But I told you. I don't know her address."

"Send it to her house here in town."

What was my dad thinking? Wasn't he listening?

"She doesn't live there anymore. What good would that do?"

"Well, for one thing, the post office will forward it to where she lives now."

"They can do that?"

"Sure. When I was in the War, I never knew where I was going to be one day to the next. But my mail always found me. Even when I was in France."

I didn't know he had been in France. Why was I finding it out just now?

"I think you should go inside and write this Violet a letter."

"Okay, I will. Right now."

"But first. Fetch the ball."

I decided to send a picture postcard instead. On the front was a picture of cars parked in downtown New Prague showing Dvorak's Grocery and Rock's Bar. I wrote:

Dear Violet,

How are you? I am fine. I miss you.

Why didn't you write like you said?

Jimmie

I mailed it to Violet's old address.

Then, again, I checked the mailbox every day for a letter.

126

After a month, I stopped waiting.

All during December, my dad got Christmas cards from his Army buddies from World War II. But I didn't get a card from Violet. Then on New Year's Eve Day, my mom came in with the mail. "Here's one for you, Jimmie."

I ran to her so fast I couldn't stop, knocking all the mail to the floor. There on top was a letter addressed to me. It was the first letter I had ever gotten! I read the return address. It was from Florida, from Violet!

As anxious as I was to read the letter, I opened the pink envelope slowly and carefully. The handwriting was in perfect longhand on pink paper.

Dear Jimmie,

I just got your postcard. I did write to you many times. But the letters were sent back, stamped return to sender.

You must have given me the wrong address.

That was smart how you sent the card to my old address.

We have moved again in Florida. I am surprised that your postcard even found me.

I hope you had a good Christmas. Please write and tell me about it. Did you get a lot of good presents?

I got a doll that is almost as tall as I am!

But that wasn't my best present. On Christmas Eve, I was sad because my grandparents weren't here for Christmas. It didn't seem like Christmas without them. Then Christmas morning, a car horn woke me up and I went to the window to look. My grandparents were in our driveway. I ran outside as fast as I could and hugged them.

They said they had a present for me in a trailer behind their car. I was wondering what it could be that was so big they needed this big trailer.

When they opened the doors, I could feel cold air. I looked inside. It was filled with snow!

They backed the trailer into our yard and shoveled the snow onto the grass. Then my grandparents and I built the first snowman ever in Florida.

Then we opened our presents inside. Every once in a while, I would look out the picture window at our white snowman on the green grass. Each time I looked it got smaller and smaller. By the time we ate Christmas dinner, it was just the size of a snowball. I went out and rescued it and he is now living in our freezer.

Happy New Year,

Violet

I read the letter at least fifty times and then started writing my letter to Violet. I didn't get anything as good as a giant doll for a present. I looked outside at the snowdrifts that came up to the windowsills. Snow that I would have to trudge through when delivering papers later in the day. How could there be no snow in Florida?

If Violet wanted more snow, I knew where she could get some.

CHAPTER 23

CRYING OVER SPILT MILK

There are plants in the lobby that seem to serve no purpose. They aren't any good for food. Instead of growing these 'weeds' in these pots, why not a tomato plant? Or sweet corn? Or mushrooms? That would make more sense.

My dad headed up the hill on Columbus Avenue toward Second Street. I usually wasn't up when the sun was just rising on a Saturday morning, but my dad wanted me along. He slowed as he neared the stop sign and pushed the clutch in. He quickly shifted to neutral and moved his left foot from the clutch to the brake. We came to a stop at the corner.

A Ballinger's Dairy milk truck passed slowly on Second Street toward its next delivery while we waited at the intersection. My dad's foot moved from the brake back to the clutch. The car rolled back a few feet as my dad stepped on the clutch and shifted the car into first gear. When he gently lifted his foot from the clutch, he pressed his right foot on the gas pedal. The car smoothly moved through the intersection continuing on Second Street toward Stepka's house.

My dad's right foot had to remain on the accelerator at all times because the engine wouldn't idle fast enough. Uncle John had supposedly fixed it the previous night. Instead of buying new parts, he tried using baling wire.

A few months ago, he had fixed the brakes just as successfully. For a week, my dad had driven to and from his job at the lumber yard, only stopping twice each time. He would slow to almost a crawl at each corner. He parked uphill at the lumber yard to make the car stop. The elm in our yard was scarred from the bumper. We knew Dad was home when we heard the hollow thump when the car hit. The house would shake a little as well as an added reminder.

"I'm taking her to the Standard Station on Saturday and get her fixed right. We can afford it now that I got the new job."

His new job was driving a can milk route. While a lot of farmers had switched to bulk, there were still farmers like my Uncle John who still hauled milk to the creamery in cans. After all, it cost money to put in a bulk cooling tank.

"You're going to be a big help to me today, Jimmie."

"I am?"

"For sure. A lot of help."

I'm glad he thought so because I wasn't so sure.

"There she is parked up ahead."

We parked across the street from Stepka's place. My dad's truck was painted a bright red but covered with a layer of mud from travel on gravel country roads and farmer's driveways. On the driver's door painted in white letters were the words, STEPKA'S TRUCKING.

"Dad, I thought you said it was your truck."

"Oh, that. The truck belongs to Stepka but it's my route."

A little disappointment entered my mind. I hoped it didn't show on my face.

"In a few years, I'll be able to buy my own truck. Maybe one of those bulk trucks."

He pointed toward a truck next to it and twice as big. The bulk tank gleamed silver in the sunlight, the cab and wheels clean. It was like the tires touched only clean dirt.

My dad opened the door of his truck and got behind the wheel.

"Get in, Jimmie. Let's hit the road."

Getting in wasn't as easy as it sounded. The running board was a big step up for a little kid like me. I managed to open the door and get in just as my dad started the engine. He backed the truck out of the yard and headed out of town toward the east, toward our old farm.

With each bump, the empty milk cans in the back clanged against each other. It was so loud I couldn't hear my dad when he said something to me.

A little louder he repeated. "First stop is Tatusek's. His cans are number forty-seven."

I knelt on the seat and looked out the back window so I could see the cans. Red numbers were painted on each can. When we had the farm, our cans were all number nineteen. I wondered who had that number now, or if they just never used that number again.

"When we get there, you get in the back and slide all the forty-sevens to me so I can unload them. Then I'll lift the full ones up to you and you can slide them to the front of the truck. Think you can handle that?"

I nodded yes. I was pretty sure about the empty cans part, but I've tried to lift full ten-gallon cans of milk without any success. Why couldn't the cans be smaller like six gallons? They would be easier for everyone to handle.

When we pulled onto Tatusek's rutted driveway, the cans jumped up and down. One empty can tipped over. The lids came off a few other cans. My dad slowed to a crawl, partly because of the cans but mostly because Tatusek's two dogs circled the truck, barking at its wheels. Our dog, Shep, knew better than to get too close to a milk truck. Some drivers didn't bother to slow down as my dad had done.

"I just know, no matter how hard I try not to, I'm going to end up with a dog under one of these wheels. Honking the horn doesn't even help."

He made it to the milk house without hurting a dog. I got out and climbed up into the back. Mr. Tatusek walked out of the milk house.

"Got a little helper today, I see."

"I hope a big help," my dad said as he took two of the forty-sevens I had moved toward him.

"When do you figure we'll start getting more for our milk? Costs almost more to make it than what I get for it."

"That's why I had to get out of farming. Somebody's making the money but it sure as hell wasn't me."

My dad lifted two full ten-gallon cans onto the truck. I could hear him grunt so even for him they must have been heavy. I tried lifting one. It wouldn't budge. With both hands on one handle, I pulled with all my weight and managed to move the can to the front of the truck, a foot at a time.

When we had loaded all of Tatusek's milk, my dad helped me off the back of the truck. I must have seemed light compared to those milk cans.

"I got one more job for you."

"Sure. What?"

"I don't want to be running over any dogs. So, when I drive out, you yell loud if any look like they're wanting to get under a wheel."

I walked along as he slowly pulled away from the milk house to the driveway. One of Tatusek's dogs followed behind like he was making sure we were leaving but gave up after ninety feet. I jumped onto the running board, opened the door, and hopped into the cab. My dad was smiling.

"Good job, Jimmie."

After a few more stops, I got the routine down. Instead of pulling the full cans on the bed of the truck, I tilted the cans and rolled them on the bottom rim. Once I got them going, they almost went where they were supposed to by themselves. I saved a couple of dogs from being run over as well.

Then we came to our old farm. The barn was painted red, but the red had faded over the years to where I could almost see our white color underneath. The ruts in the driveway seemed deeper and the weeds seemed longer. Every time I came back to our farm, it would seem smaller than the previous time. By the time I grew up, it would probably disappear entirely.

The new farmer's cans were numbered 218. It was the highest number of our route. My dad loaded two cans into the truck.

"That's it," he said.

"That's it? We used to have three."

"That's because they don't have as many cows as we did."

But we still had more milk.

On the way to our last stop, a truck filled with corn passed us. It was headed to the Green Giant canning factory in Montgomery.

"We got some time," my dad said. "Let's follow it for a while."

Within a mile, the Green Giant truck hit a bump. Green-husked cobs of corn flew off the truck. My dad stopped near the fallen corn. I jumped out and gathered the corn off the road. I searched the weeds in the ditch and found a couple more that had tried to escape.

"It looks like we'll be having sweet corn tonight," my dad said as I deposited the corn in the cab. "Get in. There's some more up ahead."

At our last stop, we had ten cans to load. I was getting good at moving the full cans in place. That's when I tried to do it one-handed. That's when I lost control of the spinning milk can. It slammed onto the bed of the truck, the cover came off and milk spilled out. I grabbed the can and lifted it as quickly as I could. The can was only half full. I thought maybe I could fill the can the rest of the way with water, but the floor of the truck was white with milk.

My dad came to the back of the truck.

"It spilled," I said.

"I can see that."

"What about the spilled milk?"

"Think you can get it back into the can?"

"No, I don't think so."

"Then there's nothing we can do about it then."

My dad didn't say much on the way to the creamery. He did say the money for the spilled milk would come out of his check. He didn't think it would be too much. I wondered how much 'not too much' was.

When we pulled up to the creamery, no other trucks were waiting to unload. My dad got up in the back and unloaded the cans onto rollers where they moved on their own toward an opening in the side of the creamery. One by one they disappeared until our entire morning's work was in the creamery being processed.

My dad pulled the truck to the end of another set of rollers. In about forty-five minutes, our empty cans emerged from another opening onto the rollers. The empty cans with their lids tipped open rolled their way toward our truck. My dad let me help stack them in place on the truck. My job was to put the lids on while he put them in order for the route in the morning.

As we climbed off the truck, Stepka appeared. My dad told me to get into the cab while they talked outside. I could hear just parts of their conversation.

"Young…"

"Riding along…"

"Spilled milk…"

"big help…"

"spilled milk…"

"good job…"

"insurance…"

"never again…"

"never again…"

Stepka walked away and my dad got into the cab.

"What did he say?" I asked.

"I guess I can't be having you help anymore."

"It's because I spilled the milk, isn't it?"

"No, it's not that. Damn, I liked it better when I was my own boss."

My dad pulled away from the creamery.

"So, it's not because I spilled the milk?"

"No, it's because of insurance and his liability if something happened to you."

But I knew it was because I spilled the milk.

CHAPTER 24

GETTING THINGS DONE

My mom wasn't herself lately. She needed more time to herself and knew I would understand. So that's why I was spending the summer at my Uncle John's farm. There was plenty for me to do there. Besides having me help with the normal chores around his farm, my uncle was showing me how he ran his sawmill.

Farmers from Dakota, Rice, and Scott Counties would haul their logs to his sawmill where he would cut them into lumber for their houses, barns, and sheds. There was so much to learn there was no way for me to remember it all. I was amazed he could remember everything.

He could look at logs as they were trucked in, and he knew if they were ash or elm or white oak or red oak. They all looked the same to me.

He said, "By the end of the summer, you'll be able to tell the difference."

"Which summer? When I'm as old as you, maybe."

We got up just as the sun rose and did the morning chores, had our breakfast of ham, two eggs, oatmeal, toast, milk, and coffee. My mom didn't let me have coffee yet, but my uncle figured one cup in the morning wouldn't hurt me. I didn't like the taste of it at first but with enough cream and sugar, I started to like it.

After breakfast, we made our way across the dew-covered grass onto the plank over Plum Creek to his sawmill. It had a large, circular blade that was wider across than I was tall. The first thing he did that morning, as he did every morning, was replace any broken teeth, broken by a nail or wire that was embedded inside a log. Carefully, my uncle examined each tooth one by one.

"This one is shot," he said.

It looked fine to me, but I did my job which was to hand him the replacement tooth. He looked at it, shook his head, and swore one of his familiar Czech swear words.

"These are the wrong ones. They're for the small blade. What did you take these out of the shed for?"

"They're the ones you told me to bring."

"Why would I tell you to bring the wrong ones? Now run back to the shed and get the right ones before the day gets wasted away."

I hurried back to the shed and grabbed a box of teeth from the shelf where he told me they'd be. By the time I got back, sweat was running down my face and into my eyes. My shirt was drenched. I sat next to Uncle John, out of breath. He was almost done putting in new teeth.

"Here's the box you wanted," I said.

"Don't need them. Turns out I had some out here all along."

I took a close look at the one he was putting in. It looked the same as the one I had handed to him earlier.

"You might as well take that box back to the shed."

Was he just trying to get rid of me? This time I took my time about it. By the time I got back, his helper, Voita Hanzel, had arrived and my uncle had already started the tractor. A huge belt was attached on one end to the pulley of the tractor and on the other to the pulley on the sawmill, with one twist in the middle to make sure the saw blade turned in the right direction.

My job was to sit on the tractor and not get hurt. There was nothing to do there but watch. But it kept me out of my uncle's way.

Voita wrapped a chain around a log and hooked it onto the harness of one of his horses. Walking along beside, Voita guided his horse toward the sawmill. At first, the log would roll as the chain unraveled, and then it would be pulled along to where the ground sloped toward the carriage. He unhooked the chain and rolled the log down the slope where my uncle caught up with it and rolled it up and onto the carriage with a large log hook. Sometimes it seemed like the large logs would almost knock the carriage off the rails.

When the log came to a stop, my uncle clamped it to two posts on the carriage with hooks. Then my uncle pushed on a four-foot-long wooden lever. The carriage and log slowly moved toward the huge spinning blade. Just before the log touched the blade, Uncle John eyed where the blade would hit the log. He pulled on a metal lever a couple of times which caused the log to move closer to him. When the log met the blade, the motor on the tractor strained as the teeth ate through the log. A thin slab was peeled off the side. My uncle pulled the wooden lever back. The carriage backed up past the spinning blade. He then pulled on the metal lever causing the log to move over an inch toward him. When the log went through the blade, a board with rough edges was cut off.

When the carriage was pulled back, he unclamped the log and flipped it over, so the now flat side rested against the upright posts. After clamping it down, he peeled a slab and another rough board off the log.

He then flipped the log, so a flat side rested on the carriage. He was then able to cut a slab and boards with no rough edges off the log.

I was amazed at the whole process. From some logs he cut two by fours, others one by sixes, one by eights, or two by sixes.

One time I asked him, "How do you know which boards to cut from each log?"

"You just know," he said. "You look at the log and it tells you."

I looked at the logs, but they didn't have anything to say to me.

After two hours, he had cut up about two dozen logs. Mrs. Hanzel appeared out of nowhere. She seemed upset about something. Voita had just pulled a log to the slope. After she talked to Voita, he unhitched the horse and they both left in a hurry. My uncle signaled me to turn off the tractor. I finally had something to do.

I got off the tractor, my body still buzzing from the vibrations. It seemed so quiet after listening to the tractor. When I got to my uncle, who was still by the carriage, I could tell he was swearing under his breath.

"Another morning shot," he said.

At least this time, it wasn't my fault.

"Might as well have some lunch," he said. It was ten in the morning. That was lunchtime. The noon meal was dinner. I turned to go toward the house. I heard a noise from up the slope. I looked up and saw a log rolling down the hill toward us.

"Uncle John!" I yelled, jumping out of the way.

He turned to look but the log was on him before he had a chance to move. He ended up flat on his back with the log on top of him.

I ran over and tried to roll the log off him. It wouldn't budge. I grabbed the log hook and tried that.

"That won't do any good. You aren't big enough to move it," Uncle John said after a few more Czech swear words. "You better go get Svoboda to help you."

He sounded like he was having trouble talking, trouble breathing with the log resting on his chest. His neighbor Svoboda lived a mile away. He might not even be home. Even if he was, it could be an hour before we got back.

"I've got an idea," I said.

"What you doing?"

"Don't worry," I said.

I ran back to the tractor and kicked the blocks from under the tires. I got on and started it up. I put it in gear. The tractor moved forward a few feet. I stopped and removed the belt. I then got back on and drove the tractor, stopping it at the top of the slope.

I picked up the heavy logging chain and dragged it down to the log. My uncle was still having trouble breathing. I wrapped the chain around the log as I had seen Voita do earlier. I then took one end of the chain and hooked it to the back of the tractor.

I got on and put the tractor in gear. As it slowly moved forward, the giant oak log rolled off Uncle John.

I ran down the hill to see how he was doing. He slowly got up on his elbows and shook his head. He reached up and straightened his cap on his head, catching his breath. He looked up at the tractor and log and chain and put two and two together.

"That was quick thinking, Jimmie." He rubbed a hand in my hair. "You might be some help to me, after all."

He pulled up his pants legs. He was bleeding from his knees and shins. He took out his red railroad handkerchief and wiped at the blood.

"We better get you to the doctor."

"Doctor. Hell. If I went to the doctor for every little thing, I'd never get anything done."

CHAPTER 25
THE LAST TO FIND OUT

My boots sunk into the manure with every step as I trudged through the calf pen. I had forgotten that a dozen calves could make this much manure. The pen was in a windowless corner of the barn; all the heat, dust, and smell were trapped inside. No wonder the calves wanted to be set free as much as I did.

The summer seemed to crawl along. I wanted to be with my new friends in town, playing baseball, riding bikes, and even working my paper route, if I had one. When I had gotten sick, the newspaper had taken my route away from me. I was hoping that the boy who took over my route, Tim Tume, might tire of it in the summer. I wanted to be in town to get it back when that happened.

Since I had 'saved' Uncle John when the log fell on him, he started to treat me less like a little kid. What had I done? It had been so much easier when I could just sit around and hold the tractor down and watch while Uncle John and Hanzel did all the work.

The calves needed dehorning. My uncle had rigged up a series of gates to form a chute. At the end of the chute, he had set up a stanchion. My job was to get behind the calves, twist their tails up over their backs as I tried to guide them down the chute, all the while standing to the side to avoid being kicked by flying hooves. It was a battle between the calves and me and the calves usually won. I kept falling in manure while the calves strutted away into the safety of a far corner.

When I was able to force a calf down the chute far enough for it to get its head through a stanchion, my uncle would clamp the stanchion around the calves' neck. He'd then grab giant pinchers and crimp off the horns. It had to hurt as the calf bellowed in pain. It was hard for me to watch as blood squirted onto my uncle's overalls and onto the cement barn floor.

One time, a calf managed to pull back after one horn was clipped and break free of the stanchion, somehow squeezing its head back through an opening too small for it to be possible. I then had to repeat the process with a calf that knew what awaited at the end of the chute.

"I don't think I'm old enough to do this," I said.

"Hell, your dad was a lot younger than you when he started helping me do this."

That was his answer to everything now. Why couldn't my dad have been a lot older when he started helping him?

Somehow with my assistance, we got the job done in twice the time it would have taken if my uncle had done it on his own.

We were headed back to the house to get cleaned up when my dad drove into the yard. At first, it looked like he was alone but when the Chevy came to a stop, I noticed my mom sitting in the back. My dad got out and rubbed his huge hand in my hair.

"You're covered in cowshit, Jimmie."

"We were dehorning calves."

Uncle John said, "Well, I was dehorning the calves. I think Jimmie was taking a nap in the calf pen."

As long as he thought that, I probably should have been taking a nap.

"Go say hi to your mom. But you can't get into the car like that. Just look in through the window."

I stepped onto the running board and tapped on the window. My mom was covered with a quilt and had a shawl around her head. She must have been roasting under all that since it was nearly ninety degrees outside. She finally noticed me and, with a lot of effort, lifted her arm and rolled down the window.

"Hi, Jimmie. You behaving yourself?" The words came out in a whisper. Just saying those five words seem to take all her strength.

"Mom. What's the matter? Are you okay?"

"I've been better. But I'll be fine. Shouldn't be too much longer. You see, Jimmie…" She ran out of breath and fought to finish the sentence.

"Too much longer for what?"

I felt my dad's hand on my shoulder.

"That's enough for today, Jimmie. I should be getting your mom home. Say goodbye now."

"Goodbye, Mom. I hope you feel better."

"I love you, Jimmie."

She rolled up the window.

"Love you, too."

What was wrong? Did she have the same sickness I had had? Did I give it to her? She was going to die, and it would be all my fault.

The car started up. I stayed on the running board, clinging on to the roof with my fingernails as the car turned around and made its way down the driveway. I peeked in the window at my mom who had already closed her eyes and was asleep. At least, I hoped she was asleep.

My dad stopped at the end of the driveway. He turned back toward me and, with a wave of his right arm, motioned me off the running board. I jumped off and watched as the car disappeared down the gravel road, followed by a whirling cloud of dust.

I walked slowly back down the driveway toward my uncle who waited, rocking back and forth on his rocking chair. The sky was a solid blue with only wisps of white edging up in the west. The only sounds were those of some crows cawing in the cornfield and the rustle of the leaves as the breeze blew through the cottonwoods. I was alone with my thoughts. My mom didn't look well. Would it be the last time I would see her alive? I wanted to go back home to be with her.

When I reached the porch, my uncle tapped his pipe clean on the heel of his boot.

"Looked like you were going to ride all the way home on the running board," he said as he dipped his pipe into a tin of tobacco.

"Can you take me home?"

"Don't you like it here?"

"I like it all right, but I'm worried about Mom. What's wrong with her?"

My uncle rocked back on his chair and put the pipe in his mouth. He lit a match on the arm of the rocking chair and lit the pipe. He thought for a few seconds as he puffed on his pipe.

"Didn't they tell you?" he finally asked.

"No, they don't tell me anything." I paced back and forth, clenching my fists. "I'm always the last to find out what's going on. Like when Uncle Vencil disappeared. Do you know what's wrong?"

"You better get cleaned up for supper. Then you need to get to bed. You have a big day ahead of you cleaning out the chicken coop tomorrow."

"You know and you won't tell me. That's not fair!" I said, now stomping back and forth on the porch.

"Maybe it's not fair. But you'll find out when you find out."

"But when?"

"When your dad tells you."

I didn't like that answer but that was the only answer I was going to get. At least, my dad was going to tell me eventually. I guess that's better than 'when you get older.' One of these days, I just might find out about things when everyone else did.

CHAPTER 26

NOBODY HOME

I saw the sign marking New Prague's city limits as Uncle John slowed down to twenty miles per hour. The speed limit was thirty. He always drove ten miles under the speed limit, just to be safe. Up ahead, I saw the huge '20' on the sign at Lexington Avenue. Sure enough, after we turned, we crawled toward our house at ten miles per hour. I had to wonder what he would do if he ever drove past our school where the speed limit was ten miles per hour.

It was Friday night, the weekend before Labor Day. Tuesday morning, I would be back at school. But today I just wanted to be home, and Uncle John was taking his time getting there. He was torturing me, unintentionally, I think. Strahan's house was on the corner; then ours was next. My uncle slowed to a stop at the end of our driveway and let me out. I grabbed my stuff from the back seat and ran toward our house.

I had missed my mom so much and I couldn't wait to see her. I dropped my things at the front step and ran into the house.

"Mom! Mom! I'm home!"

She wasn't standing at the kitchen stove. She wasn't in the living room or the bedroom when I checked there, either. She wasn't home. She knew I was coming home today, and she wasn't here waiting for me. In fact, nobody was home. I stopped running around the house and sat at the kitchen table. It was so quiet; the only sound in the house was my breathing.

I don't know why I was so upset. It wasn't like it was my birthday or anything. Then I remembered they didn't come out to celebrate my birthday this summer when I was at my uncle's place. Uncle John did his best, but it wasn't the same. I got a lot of presents from him wrapped in white butcher paper. A new hammer from Busch's Store in New Market. A new saw from Busch's Store in New Market. A new yardstick from Busch's Store in New Market. New overalls from Busch's Store in New Market. But my favorite was a pocket watch that wasn't from Busch's Store in New Market. My dad gave me a gold watch and chain from Bohemia that had belonged to my great-grandfather, Tomas.

I stomped out of the house and sat on the front steps. Where were they? But then it hit me. I had just been thinking of myself. The last time I had seen my mom she was very sick. What if something happened to her? Every time I heard a car approaching on Lexington, I was sure it had to be them. But it wasn't. After a dozen cars, I knew I couldn't just sit there and wait. I had to do something.

I got up and walked past our dying elm tree to the shed in back. I creaked open the door and looked inside. It was still there. At least, my bicycle was there waiting for me. It was covered with dust and cobwebs and the tires needed air. I had to dig through most of the shed to find the tire pump which was hiding behind some oil cans and kerosene lanterns on a cluttered shelf.

I pumped up the tires and wiped off the bike with a rag torn from one of my dad's discarded shirts. I wheeled the bike out of the shed and hopped on. I raced out of the driveway and sped down Lexington

Avenue toward Main Street, faster than my uncle had driven in his car. I turned right on Main toward the hospital. I figured if my mom was in the hospital, our car would be parked outside.

I searched the parking lot and checked all the cars on the streets. Since I didn't see our car, I decided they had just gone shopping. Our car wasn't next to Simon's Grocery or Ike's Bar. I rode past our house again. I found nobody was home, so I headed to the park. Maybe the guys would still be playing baseball since school was starting next week. Across the street from the park, I waited for a Ballinger's Dairy truck to pass and turned left. The park was empty. There weren't even any kids on the swings and slides.

I laid the bike next to a teeter-totter and walked through the sand. I took a couple of trips down the slide and spent a few minutes on the swings. Finally, I sat on the merry-go-round, a round disk about eight feet across. It had vertical bars to hang on to as you slowly spun yourself around.

The park just didn't seem to be as much fun alone as it did with Howie and Pete. I saw Pickle and Bull riding their bikes toward me from Main Street. That's when I wished I was alone. I slowed to a stop when they jumped off their bikes next to the merry-go-round.

"What are you doing on our ride?" Bull growled before I could get off.

"I didn't know it was your ride. I'll get off."

Pickle blocked me as I tried to slide off, his face so close to mine I could smell cigarettes on his breath.

"No, you didn't pay to get on. Now, you got to pay two dollars to get off," he growled, but not as well as Bull.

All my money was in my sock at home.

"I don't have any money. I'll pay you later."

"Sure, you can pay us later. Can't he, Bull?"

"Okay. But first, we have to teach him a lesson."

Bull grabbed a hold of one of the bars and started to spin the merry-go-round. Pickle raced around, keeping me from getting off. Pretty soon the wheel was going around so fast he couldn't keep up and I couldn't get off. I could hear Pickle and Bull's cruel laughter as they spun me faster and faster. I just hung on to a bar with both hands so I wouldn't fly off onto Main Street.

When I thought it couldn't get any worse, it did. I was starting to get sick. I closed my eyes as nausea built up inside me. Pretty soon I was going to throw up. Then the laughter stopped abruptly. The wheel slowed down. I opened my eyes and didn't see Pickle or Bull whirling by me. The spinning slowed enough for me to stick a leg down and drag the wheel to a stop.

I looked around and saw Howie riding Pickle's bike, followed by Pickle. Bull was chasing Chuck who was riding Bull's bike in the other direction.

I got off but even though the wheel had stopped moving, the ground hadn't. I fell to the sand and threw up. I tried to get up but fell again and threw up again. After a couple more attempts with the same result, I figured the best thing to do was just sit where I was.

I don't know how long I sat there before the world came to a stop. I got up carefully and looked around. I was alone in the park. Then I remembered seeing Howie and Chuck helping me. Why had they done that? Howie was mad at me. Why would he do anything to help me?

I walked to my bike and picked it up. I just wanted to go home, even if there was nobody there. I eased my way onto the bicycle and started pedaling. The bike tipped over almost immediately. I tried it again and fell again. Wheeling the bike next to me, I started to walk home. I wondered if I would ever be able to ride it again.

A block ahead, I saw Howie and Chuck riding bikes toward me. If Pickle and Bull were still chasing them, I couldn't see them. When Howie reached me, he skidded to a stop.

"What are we stopping for?" Chuck said when he pulled up next to us.

"How are you doing, Jimmie?" Howie asked.

"Okay, thanks to you guys."

"Us guys? What do you mean?" Chuck asked.

"You know. Taking their bikes so they'd chase you."

"Their bikes?" Howie said.

"You mean, *our* bikes," Chuck said. "We were at Ballinger's Dairy when Pickle and Bull took 'em. We chased after 'em and caught up with 'em in the park. We were just getting our bikes back is all."

"You weren't trying to help me?"

"Why would we do that? Right, Howie?"

Howie looked back and forth from me to Chuck and back to me.

"Yeah, I guess. But..." Howie finally answered.

"Come on, Howie," Chuck said. "Let's go."

I watched as they sped away laughing. Were they happy they got their bikes back? Or were they laughing at me?

I got on my bike and pedaled back toward home.

CHAPTER 27

AND THEN THERE WAS SUSIE

There are a lot of pictures on the desks in the bank lobby. Photographs of babies seem to be the most popular. But it seemed to me all the babies looked alike. It couldn't be the same baby in all these pictures, could it?

I hoped Mom and Dad were home now. The hill on Columbus Avenue, where some of my teachers lived, seemed steeper than ever before. I usually breezed up that hill. This time I had to stop a couple of times to walk my bike. I never thought I'd be slower than Uncle John.

I couldn't wait to get home and go to my room. I wanted to forget about Pickle and Bull and Howie and Chuck. When I got to our house, all I could see were cars. They were parked in the yard around the house and up the driveway. There were so many, some were parked on the street.

It must be a party. Was it a surprise party for me? Because I was home? It couldn't be that, could it? But what else would it be? Unless something happened to Mom. I remembered when Uncle Louie died, there were this many people at his house.

I leaned the bike against the huge elm in the front yard and ran inside. The house was packed with people. Noisy people. Some of them I didn't know.

"Mom! Mom! Where are you?"

But nobody heard me. Even I couldn't hear me. I made my way around the legs of the people in the kitchen. Skinny legs. Fat legs. Old legs. The young pretty legs of some high school girl I didn't know. Who were all these people and why were they in our house?

I couldn't find my mom in the kitchen, so I tried the living room. It was a little quieter there. I could hear Mom's voice. I made my way toward her. On the way, I finally met somebody I knew.

"Hi, Jimmie!"

"Hi, Aunt Mara."

"Where you headed?" Aunt Mara asked.

"Looking for Mom. Is she okay?"

"She's fine. She's sitting in that corner," she pointed. "She's been looking for you."

"She has?"

"And she has a surprise for you."

"A surprise? For me?"

I headed toward Mom. What did she have for me? The new bike I wanted. A new game. Whatever it was, it didn't matter. Mom was okay.

"About time you showed up," Dad said. He had a broad smile on his face. "We've been looking for you."

"I was out looking for you and Mom."

"Better go see her. She has something to show you. Over there."

He guided me around Aunt Rose. Then there she was. She looked skinnier and tired. But when she saw me, she smiled.

"Come here, Jimmie. Mommy missed you."

I ran up to her and was about to jump on her lap and give her a huge hug when Aunt Rose pulled me back.

"Careful, Jimmie. Your mom has been through a lot."

"She has?"

"It's okay, Rose. I'm not going to break."

My mom pulled me to her and hugged me and kissed me on my cheeks.

"I have something to show you. I want you to meet your new sister. Susie."

Next to her, Aunt Jane held a tiny baby, so small I didn't think she was real.

"Isn't she cute?" my mom said.

"Yeah, I guess. But Mom, is this why you were so sick this summer?"

"Yes, Jimmie."

If having babies made a woman that sick, I was surprised any babies were born at all.

"The doctor said I had to take it easy, Jimmie."

"But I could have helped."

"You helped by going to your Uncle John's for the summer."

Some more people I didn't know got in between me and my mom.

"She's so cute," they said in singsong voices.

I moved next to my dad. He ran his hand through my hair and put his arm on my shoulder.

"Dad, you didn't tell me Mom was having a baby."

"Yes, I did."

"No, you didn't."

"Sure. Don't you remember? I said our family was going to get bigger."

"I remember that. I thought you meant that we were all getting bigger. I'm getting taller. And Ron is heavier. And you, too. And especially Mom."

Before he could answer, Uncle Roman came up to congratulate him. I moved aside and watched as my mom kissed Susie. I felt a hand on my shoulder. I turned to see my brother, Ron.

"Now you get to see what it's like, not being the youngest."

CHAPTER 28

WHEN THE DOOR SLAMMED

"Wake up, Jimmie. I'm going to need your help today."

I woke up to see my dad's face staring down at me. It was Saturday morning and still dark out. I had been looking forward to sleeping late.

"Help?"

"Up and at 'em. Better throw on a jacket. It's a little chilly today."

I threw my legs over the side of the bed. Sitting on the edge of the mattress, I bounced up and down, trying to springboard myself off the bed. The springs squeaked beneath me. I stopped and gave myself a few minutes to rest and thought back on what had happened yesterday.

It had been my fault. I had been mad at my mom and my dad and Susie and even my brother, Ron even though he had been nowhere around. It looked bad but my dad had said it would be better today.

I slowly crept down the stairs, trying to avoid what was waiting for me in the kitchen.

"Hurry, Jimmie," my dad called from downstairs. "You afraid of a little work?"

No, it wasn't that. Not at all. I would have done anything to work with my dad. I just wished it hadn't been this.

I could see my dad at the kitchen table eating his eggs and potatoes. With the fork in his left hand, he had difficulty guiding the food into his mouth, spilling most of it on the way. His right hand rested on his knee, heavily bandaged, dried blood staining the edges of the wrap. His fingertips looked black and swollen. I don't know what hurt worse, his hand or me for having done it.

"Sorry, Dad."

"Not your fault. You didn't mean it. I just got to learn to keep my hands out of the way."

The whole night I tried to undo what had happened. I didn't know he was there. I was tired of carrying things Susie needed from the car into the house. How much could a little baby need anyway? Muttering under my breath and slamming car doors helped. Or it seemed to. Unfortunately, I slammed one of the doors on my dad's hand. I hadn't noticed that my dad had come out to help me.

Even though there was blood all over the place, even though I knew it had to hurt, my dad didn't make a sound. He didn't swear. He didn't yell at me. He just walked swiftly into the house and had my mom soak his hand in hot water and Dreft laundry soap.

"Maybe you should go to the doctor," I said as I sat down at the kitchen table. My mom put my breakfast in front of me.

"Doctor? What's he going to do but charge me an arm and a leg for my hand?" He smiled at his joke and winked at me. I knew things were going to be okay.

"What do you need me to do?"

"You're going to have to drive the milk truck today."

"Me? Drive?"

"Well, I'm going to steer and brake and everything. I just need you to shift when I push in the clutch. I'm going to have to teach you."

My mom interrupted. "I'm thinking maybe you ought to get his brother here, instead."

"No. No. I can do it. I know how to shift."

"You do?" my dad said. "Yeah, that's right. You do from driving the tractor. And I suppose I can lift the cans up with my left hand."

"I'll help you with that, too," I said eagerly.

"We'll give her a try, then." He got up holding his right hand in his left, showing the tiniest wince. It must have hurt like hell.

CHAPTER 29

FIGHTING OVER SPILLED MILK

When we left the creamery in Stepka's truck, my dad kept telling me when to shift and what gear to shift to. That's because I kept grinding the gears.

"You keep that up, Stepka won't have a transmission left. I thought you said you knew how to do this."

"I do. It's just that I'm on the wrong side."

"Yeah, I guess that would do it. Sort of like me eating with my left hand this morning."

Once we left town, my shifting chores were done, unless we had to change gears for a hill or a driveway. I looked out at Snyder's cornfield which had just been picked. Rows and rows of little corn stumps were all that was left.

"Hey, Dad! You're forgetting Simon's place!"

I looked back at Simon's driveway disappearing behind us. My dad didn't even slow a little.

"We don't pick him up anymore."

"Why not?"

"He's not taking his milk to the creamery for now."

"Why not?"

"He wants more money, I guess."

"How does he get more money if he doesn't sell it?"

"It's sort of hard to explain, Jimmie."

We turned into Kajer's driveway.

"Look there he is."

My dad pointed at Kajer's prize boar, Hector, running toward the gate nearest the milk house. "He does that every day."

My dad turned around in the farmyard and then backed up to the milk house. He got out, walked to the back of the truck, and opened the tailgate. I jumped onto the bed of the truck.

"What the hell happened to you?" Kajer asked.

"The car door won."

"Let me help you with the cans."

They lifted his five cans into the back of the truck. After the last one, I had to ask.

"Why does Hector keep running to the gate every time?" I asked, pointing at Hector, who looked like he wanted to get on the truck.

"Well, it's like this. The first time I took Hector off the farm for breeding, and we used this truck. We had the darnedest time. Took us all morning to get him on the truck. Took three of us tugging and pulling and pushing and we couldn't budge him."

My dad must have heard this story before because he covered his mouth with his hand like he was holding back a laugh.

"We finally had to blindfold him and lead him around in circles until he didn't know where he was or where he was going, and he got on the truck. Well, after he made his rounds that day, we couldn't get him off. We had to blindfold him. Now, whenever he sees this truck, well, you know what he's thinking."

My dad finally let out his laugh. So did I, even though I wasn't sure of what I was laughing at.

"We better go, Jimmie."

"You should see a doctor about that hand," Kajer added.

"It'll heal," my dad said.

"But not before you get married," I added.

The rest of the morning, we passed by a lot more driveways which we usually drove into. It seemed like a lot of farmers were making more money by not selling milk. However, we did stop at a few new farms to pick up. After Reiser's farm, we headed back to town.

"Good job, Jimmie."

"I didn't do much."

"I couldn't have done it without you. Plus, you finally learned how to stop making sawdust out of the gears."

When we made it over the last hill before town, my dad slammed on his brakes.

"This can't be good," he said.

Up ahead, three pickups blocked the road. Standing alongside, about six farmers stood with rifles and shotguns pointed at the ground. There were signs on the truck with the huge letters, NFO.

"Dad, what's NFO?"

"National Farmer's Organization."

One of the men, Simon, whose farm we had skipped that morning, marched toward my dad. He peered in through the window.

"I see you got your boy with you."

There was an uncomfortable silence as my dad and Simon stared at each other.

"We don't want any trouble. But we're going to dump your milk."

"You don't want trouble. Neither do I."

The other five men had already surrounded the milk truck.

"These farmers could lose their farms if they can't sell their milk," my dad said.

"Hell, we don't want them to lose their farms. Just want to get a better price for our milk is all. Enough farmers hold back their milk, they'll give us the price we deserve."

One farmer jumped on the back of the truck and tossed the filled milk cans onto the side of the road. The others opened the lids and emptied the cans into the grass. Soon the ditch was a creek of white milk.

"Maybe if you'd have gotten more for your milk," Simon said, "you wouldn't have lost your farm."

My dad's face turned beet red, and he made a move to open the door. He stopped when Simon quickly raised his shotgun.

"You can go now."

"Not without my cans."

Again, my dad tried to get out of the door.

"The men will throw them on," he said. "You better see a doctor about that hand."

When we got back to the creamery, Stepka was waiting.

My dad got out and stood next to Stepka who was looking at the empty cans scattered in the back of the truck.

"You finally made it here. Without the milk."

"It was the NFO. Got stopped outside of town."

Stepka looked over at me and then at my dad.

"You got your kid, I see. Maybe if you had been alone. Who knows?"

"That had nothing to do with it. They had guns."

"Yeah, I suppose. It happened to the other drivers, too. It doesn't matter. I'm going to have to let you go. I'll write you out your last check."

My dad was getting fired.

"No, you can't," I screamed.

"Quiet, Jimmie. Get into the car. It's okay."

But it wasn't okay.

I got into the car while Stepka wrote out the check. I sat and watched while my dad and Stepka talked. I felt it wasn't going to be okay for a while. And I knew it was my fault.

CHAPTER 30
NOTHING YOU CAN DO

Since I was still trapped in the bank, I decided it was time to look for money. If I was going to get arrested for being in a bank, I thought I might as well have something to show for it. I searched everywhere in the bank, but there is no money anywhere. Even when I was on our farm on Plum Creek, I was able to find coins on the ground or hiding in couches. You'd think a bank would have some money sitting around to help our family.

Things were pretty tough. My parents tried to stay in a good mood. But I could see the worried look on their faces when they thought I wasn't looking. My dad was having trouble finding another job. Even though he denied it whenever I said it, I couldn't help but feel it was my fault.

We didn't have Grandpa Joe's pension money to help out. He had moved to the Old Folk's Home last summer when I had been at the farm. Uncle John helped out the little he could, but it wasn't that much. I could tell my mom hated to accept one red cent from him.

There was Uncle Vencil and Aunt Mara. But my dad said they had fallen on hard times themselves since they had moved back to the Cities.

"We're going to have to do it," my mom said. "We have to go on Welfare."

My dad shook his head no.

"I don't want to hear of it," he said.

"A lot of people get help from the county," my mom answered.

"Well, we're not a lot of people."

"My cousin, Louise, had to go on welfare."

"Yeah. And now they can't go to the outhouse without the county knowing it."

"But sometimes you don't have a choice," my mom said.

And we didn't have a choice. We were on welfare and just had a visit from the welfare lady and her little black notebook. After she left, my mom and dad sent me outside. That was after I thought of a few ideas which I thought were pretty good. Like moving to Florida near where Violet lived. Like changing our last names. When I suggested we all become gypsies, they had heard enough, and I found myself on the front steps.

They told me to go out and play. How did they expect me to do that? I knew they just wanted to be alone so they could talk. They each had their own idea of what to do. Dad's solution was to move in with Uncle John. My mom didn't care for that idea. We had tried that before and it was a disaster. She thought we should ask her sisters for help. My dad said we weren't going to them with our hats in our hands. What was so bad about that anyway? Besides, he never wore a hat. Only caps.

"What's going on?"

I looked up to see Howie walking across the yard. He was the last person I expected to see. I got up and ran toward him. I was happy to see him. It was the first time he had been back, but I wanted to keep him away from the house. It was bad enough the welfare woman saw the mess in our house, I didn't want Howie to see it, too.

"Nothing's going on," I said after I stopped him.

"Who was that mean-looking woman I just saw?"

"Nobody."

"What do you mean nobody? She had to be somebody."

"Just somebody to see my mom and dad."

"The welfare?" Howie asked.

I didn't want to answer. I just knew he would think less of me. Although I didn't see how anyone could.

"What makes you think it was the welfare?"

"Because I heard some of the guys talking. So, was it?"

"Yes, but it's a long story."

He started walking toward my house.

"I have time. Let's go in and you can tell me."

"No," I said, stopping him. "Let's go to your house, instead."

When we got there, Howie's mom, wearing a pink dress and a clean, white apron, greeted us at the door. She had a smile on her face. She was always happy. It's easy to have a smile on your face when you don't have anything to worry about. I wondered what that would be like and wished my mom could have a smile on her face all the time. Or at least once in a while.

"Are you boys hungry?"

"No," I answered, even though I was starving. My politeness was winning out over my hunger.

"I'm hungry," Howie said. "Make something for Jimmie, too."

Thank you, Howie, my stomach said.

We sat down at the white, Formica table in Howie's clean, white kitchen. Howie's mom placed peanut butter and banana sandwiches and glasses of milk in front of us and then left us alone so we could talk. How did she know we wanted to be alone?

I told Howie the whole story. I wanted to leave out the messy parts, so he would still like me. But I didn't leave out anything. By the end, I was crying. He was too, a little, and trying not to show it.

"I don't know what to do," I said.

"I don't think there's anything you *can* do."

That's not what I wanted to hear.

CHAPTER 31
NOT ENOUGH ROOM

The next day, we drove out to Uncle John's farm. My parents had stayed up all night trying to figure out the right thing to do. They couldn't agree. So, it looked like we were going to try everything. As we neared my uncle's driveway, my mom's face tightened.

"I wish we didn't have to do this. I wish I could have gotten in touch with my sisters."

"Just as well," my dad answered. "The only thing you would have got from them is a lecture. Like always."

"If they'll help, I'll put up with anything they had to say. Alphonse said he let Evelyn know."

My dad stopped the car halfway down the driveway. When he turned to my mom his face was beet red.

"You told Alphonse! You didn't say that. Now everyone will know."

"Everyone probably knows by now anyway."

"But Alphonse. Anyone but Alphonse."

"That's the way I feel about telling John," my mom said.

My dad put the car in gear and drove up to Uncle John who was waiting in the shade under his huge, old elm. When we came to a stop, he walked up to my dad's window and leaned an elbow on the door.

"What brings you all out here?"

Of course, he wouldn't know. He didn't have a telephone, either. I sat in the back seat and listened as Uncle John listened to the story. His calm expression didn't change the whole time.

"So maybe we can all move in here, for a while. Until this all settles down," my dad said.

"I don't see how that would change things," Uncle John answered. "But you're welcome here if you want."

"I don't want to," Mom answered.

"Why don't we give it a try?"

"There's not enough room," Mom added.

"Sure, there is," my dad said. "Let's go in and take a look."

We went in and stopped at the door to each room.

"Susie could sleep here."

"We could put a bed here so Jimmie can sleep here with John. What do you think, Jimmie?"

I didn't like that idea, but I answered, "If it'll help, sure."

By the time we went through the house, my dad was shaking his head. "You're right. There's not enough room."

"I knew it," my mom said, as we went back to the car. I'm sure I saw a smile on Mom's face, for even the briefest of moments.

CHAPTER 32

THE MAGIC HOUSE

As we pulled out of my uncle's driveway, my mom sat in the back seat. The entire trip to my uncle's farm and the whole time we were at his house, Susie was in her arms. It seemed like my mom felt if she let Susie go, she would lose her forever.

I sat up front with my dad, wondering what we were going to do. With my dad not working, the welfare wanted to take Susie away. How could it get any worse?

When we reached the end of the driveway, I saw my brother's car approaching, a giant dust trail behind him.

"There's Ron," I said.

He had to be going at least fifty or sixty miles per hour. My dad always said to stay under forty on these roads. But that was Ron for you.

"It's not him," my dad said.

The car didn't even slow as it passed us, covering our car in dust.

"How did you know?"

My mom started crying in the back seat.

"What is it? Tell me."

"With all that's going on, we weren't sure if we should tell you. Your brother's been drafted."

"What's drafted?"

"To go in the Army. He's in Minneapolis for his draft physical."

"First, Susie. And now I'm going to lose Ron, too," my mom said in between sobs.

I was going to be the only one left!

On the way back home, we had to make a stop to pick up some of Ron's things. He had been staying with Novotny and Shetka since he had moved away from home. Now he would no longer be staying there.

"I wish he wouldn't've had to go in," my mom said as we turned into Shetka's driveway.

"It might be the best thing for him," my dad said. "He had to go in. Just like I did."

"But there was a war on then. Why draft boys now?"

"I guess you have to be ready for anything," my dad answered. "I heard Tupy at the VFW talking about something going on in Asia."

"Asia!"

"Yeah, Asia. Vietnam."

"Sounds like something we ordered at that Chinese Restaurant in the Cities that time we went looking for Vencil," my mom said. "And I don't think I'm going to like it any better now."

My dad came to a stop next to Shetka's porch. Both Shetka and Novotny came out the front door. They were each dressed in dirty jeans and grease-stained, white T-shirts. It was the middle of the afternoon, yet they each held a bottle of Pabst beer. They sat down on two rickety, wooden chairs and lit up cigarettes.

"Why couldn't *they* have been drafted instead?" my mom whispered under her breath.

"Heard from Tupy they were 4-F." My dad opened his door. "You stay here with Susie while Jimmie and I get Ron's stuff."

We walked up the steps into the house without Shetka and Novotny getting up or saying a word. I was pretty sure we weren't going to get any help from them carrying Ron's clothes and boxes.

The kitchen was filthier than ours had ever been. Beer cans and beer bottles cluttered the table, counter, and sink along with dirty dishes and glasses. The living room also was scattered with bottles, cans, dishes, and dirty ashtrays. Clothes covered every square inch of the floor. There weren't any dirty diapers on the floor although it sure smelled like it.

Ron's room wasn't much better. There was a small box of his things on the bed. My dad found an empty suitcase and packed it with Ron's clothes. A picture frame sat on a nightstand next to Ron's bed. I picked it up and looked at it. It was a picture of our whole family taken at a wedding last month. As I placed it in the suitcase, I wondered if we all would ever be together like that again.

By the time we got home, it was time for supper. I was so tired I just wanted to go to bed. It looked like my mom and dad were tired, too.

When we pulled into our driveway, I could see a car parked at the back of the house. When we came to a stop next to it, I saw it was the welfare lady's car.

"What now?" my mom said.

"I've had just about enough for today," my dad said when he got out of the car. He strode quickly to the front of the house and the rest of us hurried behind him. When I turned the corner, I saw the welfare lady trying to peek in the windows. A tall man in a hat, black suit, white shirt, and black tie paced back and forth in front of the house, his arms behind his back.

"Oh, there you are," the welfare lady said when she noticed us. "We've been waiting for you."

"What do you want here again," my dad barked.

"I told you I would be back. This is my superior, Mr. Ludwig."

"How do you do?" Mr. Ludwig said as he offered his hand to my father. My dad just stared at Mr. Ludwig, his hands in his pockets.

"I'd do a lot better if you all weren't here snooping around all the time."

"I'm sorry you feel that way. We just came to take a look at the house. I trust that's acceptable to you."

"No, it's not acceptable," my mom said. With that, Susie cried out, screaming. I guess it wasn't acceptable with her either.

"We have every right…" the welfare lady said.

"Maybe you do. But, please make it some other day," my dad said.

"We're here now and we'd like to see the house."

My dad marched to the top step, turned around, put his hands on his hips.

"I said, make it another day."

My mom, with Susie in her arms, scurried behind my dad. I moved next to my dad.

After a few moments of everyone just staring at each other, the tall man finally spoke.

"Come on. This can wait for another day."

"But," the welfare lady said.

"I said it can wait."

We watched as they walked toward their car, not moving until we heard their car leave our driveway. We turned to walk into the house.

"I couldn't let them in to see the house like we left it," my mom said.

When I walked in the front door, I couldn't believe what I saw. The house wasn't like we had left it. The floors were spotless. The dishes were washed and put away. The clothes were clean and folded and placed in the dressers or hanging in the closets. Even the walls had been cleaned. New curtains covered the windows.

"But how?" Mom said.

"I don't know. Your sisters maybe."

A look of horror came to her face.

"Get them back. Hurry. The welfare people. Get them back."

"We can't. It's too late. Why?"

"Because I'll never be able to keep it looking this nice."

"I'll see if I can get them back here tomorrow," my dad said.

My mom looked around and shook her head. "I just hope that won't be too late."

Then there was a knock on the door. My mom and dad opened the door to find the welfare lady and her boss on the front steps.

"I thought you left," my mom said.

"We did," the welfare lady said. "But I talked him into coming back. I convinced him he had to see the state of your house."

"Well, I guess we can't stop you," my dad said.

The lady barged in, followed closely by her boss. They stopped in the kitchen and stared. And he looked at her with a strange look on his face.

"This doesn't look like a mess to me. It's almost spotless."

"It didn't look like this before. I swear."

"I don't need to see anymore. Let's go."

CHAPTER 33

WHERE IS EVERYTHING

After the welfare lady and her boss left, my dad led the way into the living room. He stopped suddenly a few steps into the room, with us standing behind him.

"It's not right," he said.

"What do you mean?" my mom said. "The room is spotless."

"That's what I mean. It's not like our house anymore. Like I'm wearing someone else's shoes."

I knew what he meant. It reminded me of when we went to my Aunt Rose's house. I just never felt at home there, but it was okay because it wasn't our home.

My dad sat down in his usual armchair, but he didn't look the least bit comfortable.

My mom said, "If this helps us keep Susie, then it's worth it."

My mom sat on the couch, Susie asleep at her side. I sat on the steps leading upstairs but I felt like I was breaking some new rule of the house. We sat staring at each other for a few minutes, not saying anything.

"Now what do we do?" my mom asked.

"I'm sort of afraid to do anything," I answered.

After a few more moments of silence, my dad pulled off his shoes and dropped them on the floor in front of him. He leaned back and lit a cigarette. In just that short time, the house seemed more relaxing.

"Who do you think cleaned the house?" I asked.

"It had to be my sisters."

My mom took off her scarf and draped it over the back of the couch. She took off her shoes and tossed them on the floor. I expected Aunt Rose to jump out of the closet and pick everything up.

"Hmph. It's not something they'd do."

"Oh, sure they would. They've done a lot for us."

"Maybe they would do it all right. But there wouldn't be any secret about it. We'd have heard about it."

We sure would have.

"The day's not done yet," my mom said. "Oh, well. I better fix us something to eat."

She put Susie in the crib before she disappeared into the kitchen. Susie was so tired she didn't wake up, even with the sounds of pots and pans clanging in the next room.

"I can't find anything. Things aren't where they're supposed to be."

"Where are they supposed to be?" my dad asked.

"Where I last left them. That's where."

"I hope this doesn't mean we're going to starve," my dad laughed.

"No, but it might take me a while."

All during supper, at the kitchen table, my dad ate slowly, taking a long time between each bite. It looked like he wanted to say something but couldn't get it out. It wasn't like him. He never wasted much time eating. Or talking.

When we were all done, he said, "I have to get a job, that's all there is to it."

"But there are no jobs here. You looked everywhere."

"Not everywhere."

"What do you mean?"

"Duluth. I got a letter from Stash. He said he can get me in at the shipyards."

"But you'll be gone all the time."

My mom looked at my dad's empty armchair like he was already gone. From the time I can remember, my dad had spent every night at home.

"I'll get home some weekends."

"What am I going to do here by myself?"

"I'll be here," I said.

There was a long moment of silence.

"It won't be for that long," my dad finally said.

"That's what you said when you left for the Army for the war. That little while was four years."

I left the table and ran upstairs. I hoped it was still there. Even if it was, I might not find things just like my mom couldn't find things in the kitchen. I could only hope it was in the last place I left it.

Of course, it wasn't. I tore my closet apart. There was no money sock. I looked where I usually kept my dirty laundry pile. There wasn't a dirty clothes pile. There weren't any dirty clothes in the whole house.

They wouldn't have taken it, would they? Did they think they deserved it for cleaning our house? Did Ron take it again? No. He was in the Army. Where could it be? And then it hit me. The dresser! In the sock drawer.

And there it was. I grabbed it and ran downstairs as fast as I could. My dad was still at the kitchen table, running his hands through his hair. I handed him my sock full of money. My bike money.

"Here. You can have this. Then you won't have to go away."

"That's nice of you, Jimmie. But it wouldn't be enough anyway."

CHAPTER 34

TO DULUTH

The next day, my dad packed up to go to Duluth. We all walked to the Star Cafe so he could catch the Greyhound Bus. He figured the old Plymouth wouldn't make it to Minneapolis, let alone Duluth. It would have made it to the Star Cafe but there was nobody to drive it home. We were early, of course. As we sat on the bench, I knew I didn't want him to go. We just sat on the bench waiting but not talking. What was there to say?

Uncle John waited next to my dad. I knew he was against my dad going. He had heard stories about people disappearing in Duluth. I didn't know if the stories were true or not, but it made me worry that my dad might not come back.

A farmer my dad knew, Peter Kopek, came out of the Star Café. He had both a toothpick and a cigarette in his mouth. He struck a wooden match on his overalls and almost lit the toothpick. He stopped at the last second, lit the cigarette, and looked around to see if anyone noticed. He saw I was the only one, smiled, and winked at me.

"What are you all doing downtown?" he asked my dad.

"I'm taking the bus to Duluth. I got a job working in the shipyards with Stash."

Kopek shook his head and grimaced as if it was the worst thing he had ever heard.

"You aren't going to like it. It's not like farming."

"It's a job. I'm not supposed to like it."

Kopek turned to walk away, still shaking his head.

"Yeah, I suppose. Just glad it's not me going."

If I didn't feel good about my dad going before, I felt worse now.

When the bus finally arrived, my dad just sat there. Passengers slowly got off the bus. I wasn't paying attention to them because I was wondering why my dad wasn't getting on the bus. Maybe he had changed his mind. I looked up to see someone I knew getting off the bus.

"Hello, James. Did you come to meet me?"

"Sister Florida! You were on the bus?"

"Why yes, James."

"Where were you?"

I guess I just thought that nuns never left St. Wenceslaus. Never left New Prague.

"I went to Mankato to see my brother. He is in ill health, so I went to offer him comfort."

"You have a brother?"

"Why, yes, James. I have a brother."

I thought nuns were always nuns, but I guess they had to have a family and had to come from somewhere.

The driver placed a suitcase next to Sister Florida.

"Here's your luggage, Sister. Have a good day."

"And bless you for providing a safe journey."

She turned to me.

"So, if you didn't come to greet me, why are you here?"

"My dad's going to Duluth, to work."

She looked over at my dad, who was now picking up his suitcase and preparing to board the bus. He stopped at the door to the bus.

"He's waiting to say goodbye to you," Sister Florida said. "Go."

I ran to my dad. He didn't say anything. He just brushed his right hand through my hair and turned to board the bus.

It was a slow trip home. It seemed farther than when we went. It was already dark as we neared our house. I saw a car parked in our yard.

"Look, Mom!" I said, pointing at the lights in all the windows.

"Now what?" my mom said. "I wish your dad was here."

We slowly made our way to the front steps. It looked like my mom wasn't sure she wanted to go inside.

"Come on! Hurry up!"

That was my Aunt Rose's voice from inside the house. Aunt Jane stomped out the door with a mop, pail, and broom in her hands, followed by Aunt Rose.

"So, it WAS you!" my mom said.

Aunt Rose screamed and Aunt Jane dropped everything.

"It was us what?" Aunt Rose said.

"That cleaned our house yesterday."

"Yesterday, no. We thought we'd come out and help you today, but you were gone. So, we decided to surprise you. But it wasn't that bad. I don't know what that welfare lady was looking at. I hope she doesn't get a look at *my* house."

"That's because someone cleaned it yesterday."

"Really cleaned it," I said.

"Well, it wasn't us," Aunt Jane said.

"Then who?"

"I don't know. But if you find out, let me know so they can clean my house."

They loaded everything in their car and left. The house was once again spotless. I guess the secret to keeping our house clean was to leave for the day.

CHAPTER 35

THE SHOPPING SPREE

My dad had been gone for only two weeks, but it seemed more like a year. The house was starting to return to its pre-cleaned-up mess. My mom tried her best to keep it clean. I helped as much as I could. It was like she didn't know how.

My dad sent an envelope full of money from his pay at the shipyards. The short note from him said to use the money to pay the rent and the electric bill. There was nothing about loving us and missing us. He must have figured we knew it, so why waste time writing it in the note.

My mom bundled up Susie and had me get my wagon from the shed. Since my mom didn't drive, we walked downtown, pulling Susie behind in the wagon. The first stop was the grocery store where my mom bought dozens of bags of candy, four six-packs of pop, and six bags of potato chips. All of this barely fit in the wagon with Susie.

The next stop was Ben Franklin's Five and Dime. Here my mom picked out three comic books for me and three dolls and a lot of other toys for Susie. When we got out of the store, she tried to put all this in the little wagon with Susie and groceries.

"We need a bigger wagon," she said.

I just shrugged.

"We'll just have to carry these bags," she said. By we, she meant me. I had to stop at the end of each block to rest my arms. I was glad to get home. My mom went in, carrying groceries, toys, and Susie. I put the wagon away in the shed. By the time I got inside, Susie was already stuffing herself with candy and potato chips. She had too much of everything in her arms.

"We didn't pay the rent," I reminded my mom.

"Oh, that's right. And the electricity, too. Oh well, I'll just pay them with the money your dad sends next time."

Two weeks went by, and we still hadn't found out who had cleaned our house when we were gone. My aunts denied it. My mom believed them because if it had been them, they would want her to know it. And everyone else they talked to.

Uncle Vencil and Aunt Mara were too far away, now living in the Cities, to have done it.

So, who else was there? I no longer believed it could be magic, like the elves in the fairy tale, *The Elves and the Shoemaker*, who cobbled shoes while the shoemaker slept.

The next day, my dad showed up on our doorstep.

"Dad! What are you doing home?"

He ran his right hand through my hair.

His other arm was in a cast.

CHAPTER 36

THE DRAWING

I found where the bank kept the money. It was behind bars, locked in a huge safe. At least, I figured that's where it was. Pickle and Bull had a better chance of getting money by robbing the funeral home.

The rent money was due. We had already bought food with the last of my newspaper route money that I had been saving for a bicycle. Plus, the last time I collected for the newspaper, I didn't send in what I owed to the Faribault Daily News. Both my mom and dad assured me they would pay me back when my dad got a job. My dad had been looking for work but there wasn't much he could do with one arm in a cast, even if there were any jobs available.

Mr. Prokop, the landlord, had already stopped by for the late rent a few days ago. We all hid in the closet pretending we weren't home until we heard his car pull out of the driveway. My dad's car was parked under the tree outside, so I was pretty sure he must have thought we were home.

He left a note on the front door. It read, "I know you're home. If the rent isn't paid by tomorrow, action will be taken."

"What action?" I asked. "Will we all go to jail?"

"No," my dad answered. "But we might have to move."

"Oh, no. Not again," I said.

"Where to?" my mom asked. "I'm not moving to Uncle John's."

"No," my dad said. "He won't let us live with him anyway."

"Why not?" my mom said. "Aren't we good enough now? Does he want us to live in the street?"

I pictured us sitting on our couches and chairs watching television as cars sped past us. What if it rained?

"I shouldn't have spent that rent money," my mom said.

"That's okay," my dad said. "You can't cry over spilled milk. After all, how were you to know I would break my arm?"

I left them in the house and headed downtown. It was Friday night, and the stores would be packed. Farmers came into town to shop. Stores would be open until ten o'clock.

As I passed Bartyzal's Bar, eighty-year-old Mr. Vranek came out of the front door, followed by his mongrel dog, Hunyak. My dad said Mr. Vranek always took Hunyak to the bar with him. I guess Hunyak enjoyed a beer as much as the next guy. I watched as they snaked their way down the sidewalk. It's a good thing they were walking since neither of them was in any shape to drive. They crossed the street and entered Rock's bar.

Mr. Vranek usually only came to town in the morning and was home by noon. What was going on? There seemed to be more people in town than most Fridays. Cars were double-parked along Main Street. Polka music was being played over loudspeakers mounted on light poles along the street.

"Are you here for the drawing?"

I turned to see Marty behind me, excitement showing on his face.

"What drawing?"

"What do you mean, what drawing? The stores are giving away a hundred dollars."

They must be rich to be able to afford that, I thought.

"What do I have to do to win?" I asked.

"You can't win," Marty said. "Only grownups can win. They aren't going to give a hundred dollars to a kid. Every store has a box where your folks can enter. They don't even have to buy anything. Just go into the store and fill out a slip by 8:30. They announce the winner at nine o'clock."

A hundred dollars was a lot more than we owed in rent. I looked up at the clock on the St. Wenceslaus Church steeple. It was almost eight o'clock. I didn't think I had time to get home and get Mom and Dad in time to register.

"See ya," I said to Marty and took off.

"Yeah, see ya."

I ran into the first store I came to, Hruska's Hardware. I went to the counter where I saw the box. A heavy-set lady was filling out her slip. She took her time about it as I paced back and forth behind her. When she finished, I filled out a form with my parents' names.

"What are you doing, young man?" Mr. Hruska looked back over his shoulder at me.

"Entering the drawing," I said.

"Sorry. Only adults can enter. Now run along."

Embarrassed as I was at being caught, I was equally determined to be more careful at the next store. I ran out and into Bisek's grocery store. This time I grabbed a pencil and a slip when no one was looking and filled out the entry form down the aisle where no one could see me. I then went back and waited near the box until I was sure no one was around and tossed the slip inside.

I crossed Main Street and did the same thing at Gamble's Hardware. I repeated the procedure up and down Main Street. Tikalsky's. Ben Franklin Five and Dime. The Rexall Drug. Hadac Market. All three Dvorak' grocery stores. At Bill Dvorak's Red Owl, Bill caught me putting the slip into the box. But he just winked at me and kept on bagging groceries for Helen Trouba.

I still had a few more stores left. I was even going to try Hruska's hardware again when the church clock struck 8:30. I had just put an entry in at Rynda's Hardware. As I was leaving the store, I saw Mr. Rynda take the box off the counter.

Now all I could do was wait. What a long half-hour it was. I sat on the ledge in front of Tikalsky's store staring at a loudspeaker as it blared out one Czech song after another. A silage truck crawled down Main Street leaving its sour smell behind. The townspeople covered their noses while the farmers didn't even notice. Finally, the church bells rang nine o'clock, and the polka music stopped.

"Can I have your attention, please?" A voice came on over the loudspeakers.

He already had my attention.

"Thank you all for coming out this evening. I would like to thank our sponsors for our first ever Friday night drawing with the winner receiving $100. I would like to especially thank…"

And he went on to name every store in town. I didn't know we had that many stores. Some I hadn't even heard of. With all these stores and all these people, I finally realized there was no chance my parents would win.

"And the winner is…"

And that's when I heard it. My folks' names were coming out of every loudspeaker in town. They had won! I had done it!

"The lucky winners must be present to claim their prize at Tikalsky's Egg Produce by ten o'clock tonight."

They must be present. I didn't know that. I looked up at the church clock. It was already 9:23. If I hurried, we all might make it. I started running for home. Past Ballinger's Dairy. Past the playground in the park. Past Bruzek's Funeral home. Past all the teachers' houses.

I ran into our front door out of breath. Our clock said it was already 9:45.

"We have to go. A hundred dollars. Now. Tikalsky Egg Produce. Ten o'clock."

"What ARE you talking about?" my mom asked.

I slowed down and told them about winning the drawing.

"Are you sure?" my dad asked.

"Sure, I'm sure. Hurry! Let's go!"

My mom packed up Susie and met my dad and me in our car. For once, the car wasn't stubborn and started right up. My dad backed the car out of the driveway and then sped to Tikalsky's Egg Produce which was on the other end of Main Street.

Going down Main Street was the wrong way to go. All the cars from the drawing picked this time to leave. We were caught in the first traffic jam in New Prague's history.

Finally, we pulled in front of Tikalsky's Egg Produce at 9:55, five minutes to spare. We hurried to the counter, out of breath.

Then my mom said as calmly as she could, "I think we won."

She proudly told Mrs. Tikalsky our names. It sounded good because we hadn't had much to be proud of lately.

"Why, yes. You are the winners. The very first winners of one hundred New Prague Dollars."

"New Prague Dollars?"

"Yes, New Prague Dollars. You and only you can spend them in any store in New Prague."

"Well, that won't pay the rent, then."

"No, I guess it won't." Mrs. Tikalsky looked genuinely concerned.

"I was kind of hoping it would."

After what seemed like a minute where no one talked, Mrs. Tikalsky finally said, "Would you be interested in a job?"

My dad answered quickly, "Sure."

"No, this job wouldn't be for you. I see you have a broken arm, plus this job is usually done by women."

"You mean you're offering me a job?" my mom asked.

"Yes. Candling eggs. You can start tomorrow if you'd like."

"Why, yes," my mom answered. "Tomorrow."

"Well, I'll be. Your first job," my dad said.

"No. My first job where I get paid."

CHAPTER 37

OZZIE AND HARRIET

The grocery cart wouldn't fit through one of the aisles. The store must have been laid out before anyone thought there would be grocery carts. I checked my grocery list. The list didn't seem that long. It must have been all the big items because the cart was almost full.

"Let me help you with that, Jimmie."

I couldn't see Bill, the grocer, but he probably saw my reflection in the huge, curved mirror at the front of the store.

"I got it," I said. "This is the last thing."

It was the loaf of bread. If it had been the ten-pound bag of flour or five-pound bag of sugar, the bread would have been squashed. I pushed the cart to the checkout counter where Bill rang up each item on the cash register. On a few items, he closely checked each price tag twice to make sure he was entering the correct amount. But on most of them, he knew the price without looking.

As I bagged the groceries, I could see there was going to be a problem. I had thought everything would fit in one bag. So, I didn't bring my wagon. I looked at the two bags and wondered how I would get them home.

Bill told me the amount and reached out his hand for me to pay him.

"Mom said to put it on our bill."

I hated having to say that.

"Okay but tell your mom to come see me about that bill."

I felt like I was stealing as I lugged the two bags out of the door.

About a half a block from the store, I knew this wasn't going to work. The two bags were so heavy they were sliding down my body and I was carrying them a few inches from the sidewalk. So, I came up with a plan. I set one bag down and carried the other one about twenty yards toward home. After setting it down, I went back for the other bag and carried that one twenty yards past the first bag. In this way, I would leapfrog the groceries home.

"Kind of hot today, Jimmie."

I looked up to see Ozzie. He was a friend of my dad's, in his fifties. A lot of kids made fun of him. He had no legs and made his way around town in a red wagon. He had calloused hands and strong arms that looked like Popeye's arms, strong not from spinach but from propelling the wagon over the town streets and sidewalks. But he also had the help of Harriet, a huge brown dog, so huge it could have been half dog and half horse. Harriet was attached to the handle at the front of the wagon with a rope. That's why you never saw Ozzie without Harriet.

My dad had told me the story about Ozzie and Harriet. At the same time every day, they would go to Ike's Bar. Ike would help Ozzie onto a stool and pour him a tall glass of beer. Ike would then pour some beer into a bowl for Harriet. While Ozzie would drink any brand of beer, Harriet would drink only Grain Belt. What was it about the dogs in New Prague and beer?

"Yes, it sure is hot, Ozzie."

"Looks like you could use a little help."

"Oh, I can manage. I just have to hurry so the ice cream doesn't melt."

I moved another bag toward home.

"How about if you put the bags in my wagon with me and you and Harriet can pull us all to your house?"

I looked at the bags and Ozzie and the wagon.

"I don't think they'll fit."

"I think you're right on that one. How about if you help me out of this wagon and sit me in the shade of that oak tree. You could take the groceries home and then bring the wagon back to me."

"Yeah, I guess, I mean. How?"

"Come here. I'll put my arm around your shoulder."

I moved next to him. This didn't seem like such a good idea to me. Actually, it seemed like a bad idea. And I knew when all was said and done, I would know what the bad thing was.

He smelled of sweat and tobacco and aftershave. His beard scratched my face as I lifted him from the wagon. His muscular biceps pinched my neck. He swung from the wagon, and he dangled from my shoulders as I shuffled to the tall elm tree in front of St. Wenceslaus Catholic Church. He got to be too heavy, and we fell in a heap and rolled to a stop near the trunk of the tree.

He straightened himself up and leaned back against the tree. He picked up his dirty, orange, Allis Chalmers farmer's cap and pulled it on over his bald head. Harriet sat by the tree next to Ozzie.

"Are you sure you'll be okay?"

"Sure, just don't take too long, you hear?"

I ran, picked up each bag, and placed them in the wagon. Then I ran toward home with Ozzie's wagon in tow, avoiding cracks and bumps.

When I reached our house, I pulled the wagon to the front steps. I grabbed a bag and hurried into the house. After placing the bag on the kitchen table, I rushed out for the second bag. Just as I placed the second bag on the table, I heard my mom calling from her bedroom.

"Is that you Jimmie?"

"Yes, Mom. It's me. But…"

"But nothing. I've been waiting for you to get back. I have to go to the neighbors. You need to watch Susie."

"I can't. I have to get back for Ozzie. I have to get his wagon back to him. He's waiting."

"Oh, Ozzie can wait. Is he at Ike's again?"

"No. He's under a tree."

"Under a tree. What's he doing under a tree?"

"He let me use his wagon. So, he's waiting in front of the Church."

"Well, it can't be helped. I'm late as it is."

"But Ozzie," I said.

"I'll hurry back as quick as I can."

She put on her scarf and headed out the door.

"Make sure that Susie behaves."

Sure enough. As soon as she closed the door, Susie started crying. And no matter what I did, she wouldn't stop. It almost made me want to cry myself. After ten minutes of this, I heard thunder to the west.

Then I got an idea. I ran out and got a piece of twine from the shed. I pulled my wagon from behind the house and tied it behind Ozzie's wagon. I ran in and put a coat and cap on Susie. I then put her in the front wagon. This did nothing to stop her crying. It seemed to increase in intensity.

I went to the front and started my wagon train back to the tree where Ozzie waited. The movement of the wagon seemed to quiet Susie. I looked to see that her tears had turned to grins and laughter. I would have to remember this for the future.

Ozzie was laying on the ground, sleeping at the base of the tree. He was unaware of the storm rumbling just outside of town. The sky was a deep greenish-black. I would have to hurry to get back home before it started raining.

When I stopped the wagon, Susie started crying. This woke Ozzie up.

"'Bout time you got back here."

"I was afraid I wasn't going to get back to you at all."

Ozzie looked around him and then behind the tree.

"Where's Harriet?"

"I don't know. She wasn't here when I got back."

"Help me up. I got to look for her."

I unhitched the wagons and pulled his wagon over to Ozzie and bent down. He reached up and put his arms around my neck. He lifted himself off the ground and swung onto the wagon. That was a lot easier than I expected. Ozzie situated himself on his wagon.

"You're going to have to pull me around," he said.

Here was the bad thing that was going to happen. I couldn't take him to find Harriet and get Susie home, too. Especially with the storm rapidly approaching. Then I remembered I had forgotten to leave a note for my mom.

"There you are. I've been looking all over for you."

I saw Tim Rosvall marching toward us, his big, red nose leading the way.

"Where else would I be?" Ozzie said.

"Probably where your dog is. Harriet must have gotten tired of waiting for you. She's down at Ike's getting drunk. You better get her home while she can still walk."

First, Hunyak and now Harriet. Did all the dogs in New Prague drink in the bars? I wasn't going to tell Shep about this.

CHAPTER 38

INTO THE DARKNESS

"What are you doing in here? You should be out playing on a nice day like this."

"I was. I was thirsty."

"Well, go out and play before I put you to work."

"Okay."

I didn't feel like playing but it was better than anything my dad might have for me to do.

I went out and sat on the front steps. My bicycle was parked in its spot against the red oak in our yard. The tree was put there just to hold up my bike. A chipmunk rustled around in the grass out by the huge oak. It reminded me of Chubbie. When I was six years old, my dad told me a story about Chubbie the Chipmunk and how Chubbie learned to drive a car. For quite some time, I actually believed that story. I had believed everything my dad said and accepted it as the gospel truth. I wish I could believe him now, that everything was going to be okay.

I heard some boys joking and laughing. It was Howie and some of the guys, Bob, Charlie, and Tom, walking past our house, headed toward town. I remembered when they used to stop by and ask me to go along. I wished that I could live that day over again, the day I said those things about Howie. And I wouldn't say them. I could now be walking along with them, joking and laughing. I couldn't just sit on the steps all day. I decided to follow them.

They walked down Columbus Avenue and turned right onto Main Street toward downtown. Trailing about a block or two behind, I tried to stay out of sight as much as possible, hiding behind trees and parked cars. They passed Ballinger's Dairy, the New Prague Times office, the Post Office, and the First National Bank. They stopped in front of the movie theater. None of them saw me as I waited a few doors down in front of Bisek's Grocery. For the first time, I noticed they each carried flashlights. Howie rapped on the door.

DJ, whose dad owned the theater, was a tall, high school kid about four years older than us. DJ opened the door and looked up and down Main Street and then ushered Howie and the four others inside. It seemed like everyone in school liked him. He also found the time to hang around us younger kids. DJ knew the most interesting places in town.

What was DJ showing Howie and the others? I was dying to know. We had all been in there with him last year when DJ showed us the projection room, the day after an old Czech film caught fire, destroying one of their projectors. DJ said it must have been a real hot movie. He always knew how to make us laugh.

I hurried down the sidewalk until I reached the theater. I cupped my hands and peeked inside. No one was visible. Where did they go? I tried the door, expecting it to be locked. It wasn't, so I sneaked inside.

The smell of popcorn filled the air. Under the glass counter, M&Ms, Snickers, Hershey bars, Dots, almost every kind of candy was displayed. If I were DJ, I would have a tough time keeping myself from sampling all that free candy.

I heard the sound of voices coming from inside the auditorium. I tiptoed across the lobby over the plush, floral carpeting over toward the one opened door to the seats. It was dark inside the theater, but I saw beams of light from behind the last row of seats. I stopped in the lobby before going into the theater and listened.

I heard some mumbling and whispering.

"I'll go first. Then you can all follow. Okay?" I heard DJ say. Where were they going? Then I heard the sound of feet banging against the seats. Finally, I heard the muffled voice of DJ.

"Who's next?"

"I'll go."

That was Bob. I got up the courage to look inside. The three remaining guys stood behind the last row of seats, aiming their flashlights down into a three-foot by three-foot hole. They were so concerned about what was down there, they didn't notice me. Then Charlie climbed down into the hole. I watched as Tom followed close behind. I waited for Howie to go in next. But he just stood there, looking down into the hole for about a minute.

"Hey, Howie. Where are you?"

"I, ah, I changed my mind."

"What's the matter? You chicken?" Tom laughed.

"No, I just changed my mind, is all. I'm heading home."

I quickly ducked behind the door. I could hear laughter and catcalls coming from under the seats. I expected Howie to rush by and out of the theater any second. I hoped the sound of my breathing wouldn't give me away. But Howie never came out. Finally, after a few minutes, I heard Howie clamber down the hole.

I just had to find out what was down there. The flashlights the ushers used were kept on a shelf by the popcorn machine. I hurried across the lobby and grabbed one.

I ran into the theater and crawled behind the last row of seats. I switched the flashlight on and aimed it down the hole. A tunnel that led from the rear of the theater, sloping downward toward the front, appeared in the beam of light. Something was keeping me from crawling into the tunnel. I didn't think I would be afraid of going down there. This is what Howie had been going through. My mind was headed home but my body was edging its way down through the trapdoor.

The tunnel was even smaller than it had looked. There wasn't enough room for me to crawl on my hands and knees. The only way to move was to pull myself along on my elbows, dragging my legs behind. It also meant there was no turning back.

I crawled along, moving inches at a time. A few times I tried to get on all fours. Each time I bumped my head or scraped my back. It was difficult to get a sense of time or distance down there. How long had I been in the tunnel? How far had I gone?

Then I heard someone screaming in the tunnel ahead of me.

"Help!" I heard Howie yell. "Help!"

What was happening? Was he hurt? Is the tunnel collapsing? My first instinct was to escape, to go back. But I couldn't even if I had wanted to. Besides, Howie sounded like he was in trouble and maybe I could help. I tried to yell but nothing came out. Again, I tried to crawl on my hands and knees. Again, I banged my head. This time I dropped the flashlight. Even worse, it went out. It was pitch black. I had never been in a place so completely dark before. I could hear myself breathe.

I groped around, feeling for the flashlight, and scraped my fingers on a nail that stuck out from the tunnel wall.

"Help! Somebody help!" Howie screamed.

"It's okay, Howie. It's Jimmie. I'm behind you."

"You are? Hurry!"

How was I going to help? I was completely in the dark.

I moved forward about a foot. There in front of me, I felt the flashlight. I picked it up and flicked the switch on and off and on and off. It was still dark. Then I did what my dad would do. I banged the flashlight against the wall a few times. Miraculously, it came on.

"I'm coming, Howie."

"Hurry!" he answered.

I made my way down the slope of the tunnel. Every so often Howie would yell for me to hurry, and I'd yell back that I was coming. Finally, I saw him up ahead. It looked like his flashlight was turned off.

"I see you, Howie! How come you're lying in the dark?"

"My flashlight battery died."

"Did you bang it against the wall a few times? It should work. It always works."

"This time it didn't. I'm glad you're here. But how did you know I was down here?"

"I followed you."

"Good thing. I'm caught."

"Caught?"

"Yeah. On a nail. And I can't reach back to unsnag it."

"Just hang on. I'm almost there."

"I'm not going anywhere. I can't believe they left me."

"They probably thought you went home."

"Yeah. That's right."

I crawled up behind him and saw where he was snagged.

"It's not a nail. It's some kind of hook and it's got your belt loop."

"Can you get it out?"

"I think so."

I reached over him with one hand. It took me a while, but I was finally able to pull the belt loop back, freeing Howie from the hook. Howie sensed that he was free almost immediately and his whole body relaxed.

"Ah, that's better."

"You crawl forward, and I'll shine my light ahead of you."

Slowly, we inched our way down the tunnel. After what seemed like forever, Howie said, "Doesn't this tunnel ever end?"

"It looks like we're not going downhill anymore. We must be close."

We crawled a little more.

"There it is. I see a door up ahead," he said.

We moved faster just in case the door decided to move farther away. When we reached it, Howie grabbed the handle and pushed. Nothing happened.

"It won't move," Howie said. "I think it's locked!"

"You mean, we're trapped?"

"I think so."

We were both silent for a moment. I shined my flashlight on Howie to make sure he was still there. Howie started yelling for help as loud as he could and pounded on the door. The sound echoed throughout the tunnel, and it was so loud it hurt my ears. Somebody had to hear us.

"Wait. Wait. Let's listen," I said.

Nothing could be heard outside the tunnel.

"What if no one comes? How long can we last down here?"

"A while, I guess. Just so we don't run out of air."

Howie closed his mouth and held his breath. His cheeks puffed up. He then began pounding on the door again, yelling and screaming. That's when I started to panic, too. Maybe we might die down here. No one would find us until it was too late. How many movies would people see, not realizing we were down here?

I joined Howie, yelling and screaming.

Howie couldn't use his shoulder to ram the door, so he banged his head against it in between screams.

Then he stopped.

"It's no use. They'll never find us."

"Sure, they will. There's a movie tonight. Someone will hear us then."

"If we make it that long," Howie said. I could tell by looking at him, he had lost all hope. He had given up.

"Howie, you wait here. I'm going to crawl backwards to the other end. I should be able to get out that way."

"I'll crawl back with you."

"No sense both of us going. When I get out, I'll get someone to open the door."

"But we only have one flashlight! You aren't leaving me alone in the dark!"

There was that. The thought of crawling back in the dark didn't appeal to me.

"How about if you shine the light back into the tunnel? That should give me enough light."

At least, I hoped it would.

I inched my way backward. It was a lot harder than going forward, which was hard enough as it was. My pants and shirt crept upward, leaving my legs, stomach, and chest bare. The rocks from the gravel floor of the tunnel dug into my skin.

After a few yards, I backed up the slope of the tunnel. That made it much more difficult and painful. It was getting darker the farther I crawled. The light from the flashlight wasn't able to turn the corner uphill.

"Are you there yet?" Howie yelled.

"Almost!" I answered, even though I knew I had a long way to go.

Soon, the light faded away and I was creeping along in complete darkness. I couldn't tell how far or how fast I was moving. For all I knew, I might not be moving at all. Like treading water on dirt. Where was the other end of the tunnel? Had I taken a branch off the tunnel that I hadn't known about and was now crawling under all the buildings and houses in town?

Then the bottom of my right foot banged against something solid, taking me by surprise. I had reached the other end. In the pitch darkness, I reached up and felt for the trap door. When I found it, my heart started pounding faster and faster. Pretty soon, we would be out of the tunnel and in the fresh air outside.

But when I pushed up on the door, it wouldn't budge. With all my weight and strength, I leaned into the door.

It didn't move. This door was locked, too. Now I started to think we might not get out of there. I decided to crawl back down and join Howie. This trip seemed much faster and easier than going backward uphill. Eventually, I saw the light of the flashlight.

"Is that you?" Howie asked. He must have heard me in the tunnel.

"Who else would it be? Yeah, I'm coming back!"

"Coming back! You couldn't get out!"

"Hang on. I'm almost there."

That didn't calm him down at all. It didn't calm me down, either. The tunnel leveled off and I could see him at the end. I moved up next to him and collapsed on his legs. That seemed to quiet him down a little bit.

"I'm sorry," he said.

"That's okay. Try the door again," I said.

"That won't do any good. It's locked."

"Try it anyway."

Instead, Howie yelled again, "Help! Help!"

"Hey!" he said. "Someone's opening the door!"

It swung open. There, looking down at us, was George, DJ's dad. I don't know who got more scared. George or us.

"What are you two doing in there? Get out!"

He didn't have to tell us twice. He helped us into the dimly lit room below the stage. It was filled with air. Damp, musty air, but there was a lot of it. I didn't know that breathing would ever feel this good.

"How did you get in there?"

Neither of us answered as we looked at the costumes and scenery that were no longer used and stored below the stage. Anywhere but at him.

"Oh, it was DJ, I bet! I don't know what makes you kids do the things you do."

Neither did I.

"We thought it would be fun," Howie answered.

"It doesn't sound like fun to me," George said, shaking his head.

"It wasn't," I said. "It sure wasn't."

George finally laughed.

"It's a good thing I happened to be coming down here and heard you yelling. If I hadn't unlocked that door, who knows? Who knows what would have happened? Can you imagine if someone at the seven o'clock movie had heard you two down there? They probably would think the place was haunted."

If we hadn't made it out, it just might have been haunted.

CHAPTER 39

MYSTERY SOLVED

One day when we arrived home, I saw three cars parked in our yard. They didn't look like they belonged to anyone we knew. They were new and didn't have a speck of dirt on them. Just seeing the cars parked next to our house made our house look even worse.

"Now what?" my dad said.

"I sure hope it isn't the welfare people again," my mom answered. "With me working, the house is messier than it's ever been."

"Well, let's go in and face the music," my dad said.

When we entered the porch, there was no music. Monsignor Stepek, the pastor of our Church, stood near the front door. Seven ladies were seated on our dirty chairs. I already knew one of the ladies, Howie's mom. The others I had just seen at Church. Howie's mom was the first to speak.

"I hope you don't mind. We thought we'd just wait here until you got home this time."

"This time?" my mom said.

"Yes. The other times we had to hurry. Something had to be done."

"We had to go in and clean," another lady said.

"That was you?"

"What makes you think it's okay to go into someone's house like this?" my dad said.

"We waited for you to come home. But it was an emergency."

"What emergency?"

"We heard the welfare was coming to look at your house. And we didn't want you to lose your kids."

Kids? I thought it was just Susie. The welfare was going to take me away, too? Could they do that?

"So, you cleaned our house?" my mom said.

"Yes. We had to. But we stopped by today to tell you we aren't going to do that anymore."

"Good. I knew where everything was before. I had a hard time finding things. I never did find where you women put some of my stuff," my mom said.

"We put them where they belonged," a lady in a red dress answered.

"I still haven't found my favorite blue shirt," my dad said.

"That old thing. I threw that away."

"I knew it!"

"Like I said. I put it where it belonged."

"Be quiet, Ethel. A woman has a right to keep her house as she sees fit."

"That's what I thought," my mom said.

"But with a new baby in the house, it must be clean," said the lady in red.

Howie's mom stepped toward my mom.

"We've been talking. We believe it's impossible for anyone to keep this house clean."

"That's what I always thought, too," my mom said.

"So, we've found you a better house."

"We can't afford a better house. We can't even afford *this* house!" my dad finally said.

"We've thought about that, too," Howie's mom answered.

Monsignor Stepek finally spoke up.

"A member of our Parish has passed away and has willed his house to the Church. We talked it over with the Parish and we are willing to rent that house to you for whatever you can afford."

"Why would you do that?" my dad said.

"If it was up to me," the lady in red said, "we wouldn't be doing it."

"I didn't ask you to do it," my dad said.

"Be that as it may," Monsignor Stepek said, "the Parish has no need for the house."

"I don't understand why you're doing this for us. My wife and I don't even go to your Church."

"But Jimmie does. And hopefully, your baby, when she gets older."

"It all seems too good to be true," my mom said.

"No," my dad said. "We won't accept your house. Unless we can buy it from the Church."

"But we don't have the money," my mom said.

"There is a way. I'll work it off. You'll be needing a janitor soon. Old Harry is going to retire. He told me the other day. I was going to ask you about the job."

"But your arm. And what do you know about being a janitor?" the monsignor asked.

"Let me work with Harry for a few weeks. I'm sure I can do the job."

"He can fix anything," my mom said.

"By then my arm should be healed."

"That is an offer I cannot refuse," the monsignor said.

"There is one more thing. You forgot to tell her about it," the lady in red said. "You've got to keep the house clean."

"I knew it. It *was* too good to be true. You know I can't do that."

"That's why we're going to help you. Each night, one of us seven will come in and help you and teach you a few things we've learned over the years. Pretty soon, you'll find out you won't need our help at all."

"But I have my job candling eggs. How can I do both?"

"Some of us have other jobs, too. And, as I said, we'll help you out. If you agree, we can move you in as soon as tomorrow. As a bonus, the house is furnished so you won't have to move your furniture."

"What about this place?" my dad asked.

"I think it should be burned down," my mom said.

Everyone laughed.

"I couldn't agree more," the woman in red said.

CHAPTER 40
THE WAY OUT

Fear makes you feel like there is no way out. Maybe there was a way out. I just hadn't found it.

I couldn't just sit there in the bank and do nothing. I went into the basement to find a way out. I shined the flashlight up at the window Bull and Pickle had shoved me through. It was too high for me to reach. I tried moving a filing cabinet over to the window, but it was too heavy for even grown men to move.

I looked around the basement and found a pile of boxes in a corner. These I found I could move. Using a dozen boxes, I made a staircase up to the window. I dashed up the boxes and pulled on the window. It wouldn't open. I tried pushing. That didn't work, either. It was jammed shut. Bull and Pickle could have left it open for me.

If I couldn't get out, maybe the best thing to do was hide. There were a lot of places for a little kid like me to hide. But there was no place I could hide where they couldn't find me.

The next morning, I woke up when I heard people talking and laughing outside the bank. Then the sound of a key opening the door to the bank. Now I would find out if my lie would work. They probably wouldn't believe me if I told them the truth about Bull and Pickle. And if they did, what would Bull and Pickle do to me if I got them in trouble by squealing on them? No. The lie was my best chance.

When the door opened, a well-dressed man found me on the floor in tears.

"Young man! What are you doing in here?"

I had planned to tell him he locked me in. That I was in the bank yesterday and I had to go to the toilet. I found one downstairs. And when I got back upstairs, everyone was gone. The door was locked, and I couldn't get out.

Before I could answer, a woman with white hair entered the bank and knelt down to me. She took me in her arms.

"You poor, little boy. How horrible for you," she said. "Your parents are worried sick."

"They are?"

Of course, they would be worried because I hadn't come home.

"The police have been searching all over town for you," she said. "Were you locked in the bank all night?"

"Yes," I answered, which wasn't a lie. "I tried to get out the basement window, but it was locked."

The gentleman said, "How terrible for you. But why didn't you just call the police on the telephone."

"Wouldn't they just arrest me?"

"They wouldn't arrest you," the lady said. "After all, we locked you in here overnight."

"Why didn't you call your parents?" the gentleman asked.

I couldn't tell him my folks didn't have a phone and I didn't know how to call.

"I guess, I didn't think of that."

I had been worried all night for nothing.

214

EPILOGUE

UP IN SMOKE

About a week after I wasn't arrested, we moved to the new house. I had to make one more visit to the old house. I couldn't stay away. I tried but I had to see for myself.

Three police cars blocked off the streets by our old house. Two fire engines crossed our yard and parked, one on each side. Firemen climbed off the trucks. The fire chief barked out orders. Some men took axes off the sides of the trucks while others began unwinding hoses.

Pete, Marty, and I sat on the curb across the street, watching with what seemed like half the town. Bull leaned against a light pole, smoking a cigarette. Pickle opened a can of Copenhagen and fingered a pinch into his lower lip.

"The firemen don't seem to be in any hurry," Pete said.

"Why should they hurry? There's no fire," I answered.

"Not yet," Pete said. "How do you feel about them burning down your old house?"

"Should have been burned down before we moved in. We'd have been better off living in a barn."

"I hope you didn't forget anything in there," Marty said.

"What could I forget? I don't have anything worth anything."

"You remembered your baseball glove, didn't you?"

"Sure. I couldn't leave that behind."

"Look. There's Howie," Pete said.

Howie approached us from a block away. Since we had been trapped in the tunnel together, he had started talking to me, even when his other friends were around. Maybe he had finally forgiven me for blaming him for stealing the newspaper money.

"The sock money!" I said.

"What sock money?" Pete asked.

"My newspaper money I kept in a sock. My folks paid me back. I forgot it."

"In the house?"

"Yes. It's still up in the closet. I've got to go get it!"

"You can't! It's too late!"

"There's still time, I think."

I ran past the police cars toward our house.

"Hey! You! Come back here!" Police Officer Ziska shouted.

I ignored him and ran across the yard. I saw a wisp of smoke from the back of the house just as I reached the front door. The closet was at the front of the house. I still had time. I darted through the porch door. A fireman reached out to stop me and missed.

"You can't go in there!"

"It's my house! I forgot my money!"

"Get back here!"

216

When I got to the kitchen, there was a little smoke but no fire. I ran up the stairs toward my bedroom. When I reached the top step, all I could see was smoke. There was less smoke near the floor, so I crawled along the floor toward my closet. I could hear the footsteps of firemen coming up the stairs behind me. I reached the closet just as the fireman got there.

"I need to get you out of here, son."

"My money. Up there. In a sock."

That's the last thing I remembered until I woke up near the police cars. I was wearing a mask and was covered by a blanket. A nurse was checking my blood pressure.

"You should be fine now. Just sit here and relax," she said, with a smile.

"Did they find my money?"

"No. They didn't," she said.

"No money is worth that," Ziska said. "I should arrest you. You could have been killed."

I looked up toward the house. Flames jumped out of my bedroom window. The bedroom where I had just been. What had I been thinking? Pete and Marty sat down next to me.

"Now I've seen everything," Pete said. "Running into a burning house like that. Now I've seen everything."

"I thought you were a goner," Marty said.

"He *is* gone. Gone crazy," Pete said.

Howie rode up next to us on his bike.

"Why did you do a stupid thing like that?" he said.

"All I could think of was my newspaper money. And it wasn't even there," I said.

"That's because I have it. A bunch of us snuck in there last night. And I found it. I was going to give it to you but then you went running into the house."

"You've got it?"

"Yes. This time I did take it. Now we're even."

"Look at that!" Pete said.

Pete helped me up and pointed toward the house. Flames had now engulfed the entire house. I heard screeching from inside.

"There goes another one!"

A rat scurried out of the basement window and ran out across the field toward Novotny's woods.

"And another one!" Marty said.

"Now I've seen everything!" Pete said, again.

Soon dozens of rats streamed from the burning house.

The four of us watched as the house burned to the ground.

"Let's go," I said. I turned away from the house. "I've seen enough."

"Yes, we've seen enough," Howie said. He put his arm around my shoulders. "Let's go over to my house, Jimmie."

I agreed. Any place was better than here. When we got to his house, he went into his garage and wheeled out a new bicycle.

"How do you like my new bike?" he asked.

"A new bike. What was the matter with your old one?"

"Nothing. My dad just decided to buy me a new one."

"Wow. You're lucky to have a dad like that."

"I don't know. He buys me things because he's never around. Not like your dad. And that bike you have. My dad never made anything for me."

I always thought Howie had everything, but I had something he didn't.

"What happened to your old bike?"

"That old thing. If you want it, you can have it for nothing."

His old bike was new enough for me.

"I can't take this," I said. "But here's my sock money. I'll buy it from you."

"Deal. Let's ride to the Star Café," he said.

We rode side-by-side. When we got downtown, Pickle and Bull were holding up a wall of the restaurant.

"What do we have here, Jimmie?" Pickle said. "A new bike? What? Did you rob a bank?"

"Shut up," I said.

"I could use a new bike. Right, Bull?"

"This is my bike and you're not taking it."

"I'm not, am I?"

"No. And from now on, leave me alone. You're not pushing me around anymore?"

"Is that so?" Bull puffed. "Who says?"

"We do," Howie said.

I turned to see Pete, Marty, and Tom standing beside Howie.

"Right," I added. "We do."

Pickle and Bull backed off and disappeared down Main Street. The five of us went inside. We each took a stool at the counter where Tillie waited on us.

Now, it was no longer what it wasn't. Now, it was home.

THE END

MY NEW YORK STORY

Up ahead, the highway transformed into false pools of water, as the hot, summer sun appeared to melt the black tar road. Magically, cars emerged from the mirage, reforming themselves from jello-like masses into solid, shiny metal as they neared. The 1938 John Deere chugged along, laboring to pull the elephantine threshing machine along at five miles per hour. Huge puffs of black smoke billowed from the smokestack at each slight incline in the road. The iron lugs of the gigantic tractor wheels dug into the softened tar as did the metal wheels of the thresher, leaving a Morse code, snake-like trail in the road behind.

My Uncle John didn't care about all of this as he steered the John Deere, his muscles straining at the wheel. The only power-steering available was human power. I balanced my small, skinny eleven-year-old body on the fender watching as beads of water dripped off my uncle's face onto his already sweat-drenched blue work shirt.

My uncle was a man on a mission, getting the rig from New Market to New Prague in the shortest time. He knew the shortest distance between two points was a straight line. It didn't matter to him that the straight line was State Highway 21.

"You want to drive?" my uncle asked, turning to face me.

"What?" I couldn't believe my ears. My heart raced. I had dreamt of this moment, envisioning myself behind the wheel. But even I hadn't thought it would be possible for a lifetime, until I was fifteen or sixteen, at least.

"Sit here," Uncle John ordered as he moved back to make room for me. I jumped from my spot on the fender to stand behind the wheel. My small fingers barely fit around the wheel as I gripped just below the huge ruddy hands of my uncle.

"Got a hold now?"

"Yeah, I think."

Uncle John slowly released his hold and let me fight the wheel of the John Deere. The tractor seemed to have a life of its own, a life which I tried to tame. The front of the tractor edged toward the centerline. I steered the other way. The monster had other ideas as it moved even closer to the other side of the road. I looked back for help, but my uncle made no moves. I put both hands on the right side of the wheel and pulled down with all my weight, lifting my feet from the floor of the tractor. The John Deere gradually turned to the right and out of the path of an oncoming '52 Chevy. I looked back toward my uncle. We each had a smile on our faces.

The tractor now headed toward the ditch. I held the left side of the wheel and with all my weight steered to the left. I continued this procedure for about a quarter of a mile. Then I heard a siren. My uncle quickly lifted me from behind the wheel to my spot on the fender.

Off to the left, a highway patrol car with red lights flashing slowed to the speed of the John Deere. A red-faced patrolman pointed Uncle John to the side of the road. My uncle pulled the rig to a stop as the patrolman positioned his car in front.

The baby-faced young officer slid out of the car and self-importantly marched back to the tractor. He didn't attempt to hide the smirk on his face as he shook his head in disgust. He came to a halt and looked up at my uncle.

"You can't be driving this contraption on this road."

"Who says," my uncle shouted over the roar of the John Deere.

"It's the law!"

"Bullshit! I was driving on this road before you was even born. Now you better move your car because I'm coming through."

"What?" It was the only response the officer could muster.

Uncle John revved the engine and shifted into gear. The rig slowly moved forward.

"You can't!" The patrolman looked to his car which was no match for the John Deere and thresher. He turned on his heels and started for his car.

"Okay. But don't drive down the main street of town!"

My uncle looked toward me. From the look on his face, I could tell he was going to do as he planned. He had told me when we started. He was going to parade his rig down Main Street of town like he owned the place.

That was the story I submitted to an editor of a magazine in New York. The editor sent the manuscript back to me in two months, along with a rejection letter and surprisingly a few suggestions. He felt the readers wouldn't relate to the story. Most wouldn't know what a John Deere tractor was, let alone a threshing machine. The story was not contemporary. The 1950s were of no interest to anyone anymore. I decided to take his suggestions to rewrite the story.

The hot, summer sun was barely visible through the smog covering the New York City skyline. From an alley ahead, a car lurched out into the street and careened toward us, magically holding itself together. The front bumper dangled precariously from one fender. The muffler dragged on the pavement. Its deafening scraping could be heard over the stereo playing in Uncle John's taxicab. Little seven-year-old, Spike sat in the passenger seat looking vacantly at the garbage-littered streets, completely ignoring his uncle. John, steering the car with one hand and flipping through his collection of CDs with the other, raced through the narrow streets at fifty miles per hour. Even though the shortest distance from point A to point B was a straight line, John snaked his way in and out of traffic, detouring to avoid overly congested areas. The faster he could get from Newark to downtown Manhattan, the more money he would make.

People on the streets were sweltering in the heat, mopping their foreheads, and perspiring through their suits and white shirts. John's Hawaiian shirt draped coolly from his narrow shoulders and skinny biceps as he lit another Marlboro.

"Hey, get ova here."

"Who? Me?" Spike asked.

"Who ya think I'm talkin' to? The goddamn doorknob? Get up here and drive."

Spike hated this. He dreaded having to drive while John worked on his trip sheet. It was the only reason he dragged Spike along. He wouldn't even move back to allow Spike space to squeeze behind the wheel. Before Spike's hands were on the wheel, his uncle's hands had already reached for the clipboard. Spike easily turned the wheel. Too easily, in fact. One second, the car headed across the centerline toward a city bus. With the slightest turn to the right, the car dove for an elephantine garbage truck parked on the right along Second Avenue. John never glanced up.

They maintained the fifty-mile-per-hour pace for ten blocks. Spike heard a siren. John quickly jerked him from behind the wheel.

"What the hell you doin' ya little shit?"

A New York City policeman pulled next to the cab and motioned John over to the side of the street. John did his best to ignore the officer for almost two blocks. He glanced over toward the policeman.

"Who? Me?" he mouthed through the closed window.

The cop angrily pointed to the side of the road. After John pulled over, the officer parked his vehicle behind the taxicab. The young fresh-faced patrolman exited the squad car and stood behind the cab, taking down the license number. John squirmed in his seat, looking in his rear-view mirror.

"Hurry up, you little twerp. I ain't got all goddamn day."

The officer slowly sauntered next to the cab and peered into the window.

"You took your sweet time pulling over."

"I didn't know you was talkin' to me."

"Who did you think I was talking to? The doorknob? You can't be driving that fast through here."

"Why not?" John asked as innocently as he could.

"Because it's against the law. The speed limit is thirty here."

"Hell, I was driving fifty through here before you was even born. Now get back in your car and let me earn a living."

John made a move to put the car in gear. The officer had his gun drawn before John's hand touched the gear shift lever.

"Hold it right there! Out of the car!"

The young cop was joined by his partner. It took two of them to pull John out of the car. The young cop read John his rights, handcuffed him, and bent him over the hood of the car. The cop then looked over toward Spike.

"Leo. Grab the kid and take him to Juvenile."

Spike opened the door of the cab and jumped out of the car. He darted down the alley. Leo gave chase until Spike ran down the steps to the subway. Within minutes, Spike was aboard a train, headed toward home. God, how he hated John. How he hated this city.

I submitted this story to the same editor. Surprisingly, within four weeks, I received a response. Not surprisingly it was a rejection letter. It did have some comments. It read:

"Timely and contemporary. Would be of interest to our readers. However, it is apparent you do not know the subject matter. My advice would be to write about what you know."

THE END

ROAD TO HEAVEN

The dew-covered grass glistened in the moonlight as Louie emerged from the back door of an old, two-story brownstone in the heart of New Market. The residents of the tiny village were still in their houses, the streets free of traffic. The screen door slammed shut, breaking the Sunday morning silence. Louie hiked up his pants and started across the lawn, leaving footprints in the grass behind him. The moisture seeped through his well-worn work boots, soaking his socks and chilling his feet. He could see by the large clock shining brightly on one of the two dark steeples of St. Simon's Catholic Church that it was almost five-thirty. Minutes, hours, days even years flew by. There was nothing Louie could do to slow time down. It was 1935 already, which didn't seem possible.

Louie was a short man, still slim and boyish in appearance for his thirty years. He wore denim jeans rolled up into a three-inch cuff, exposing all of his white socks and boots. A black suit coat covered a black tie and white shirt with a collar which was askew. Louie lifted his frayed hat and ran his fingers through his hair, combing the stray curls in place.

There was nothing like a Sunday morning after the night before. He couldn't understand why everyone was still in bed, sleeping during the best time of the day. Of course, any time he was awake was the best time of the day for Louie.

He hunched up against the cool, fresh morning air and crossed the street. He again looked up toward the towering church. What a waste, he thought. So much money spent to build something that was used only a few hours a week. It seemed a shame he would have to sit inside for hours, losing the best part of the day. People just didn't realize what was important in life. You had to live each moment to the fullest. And Louie usually did just that.

He had enjoyed himself the previous night. Everyone in New Market liked Louie; he was the music, the laughter, and the excitement in every gathering. On his concertina, he could play any song requested as long as it was one of the hundreds he knew. He could tell story after story that would leave an entire room in tears of laughter. There was a fire in his eyes and intoxication in his voice. The electricity of his presence brought others to life. Long after almost everyone else had succumbed to fatigue and exhaustion, Louie would still be going strong.

Wanda had almost outlasted him. She was new to the area. Louie had met her for the first time last night. He had enjoyed her company and they seemed to complement each other. Her flaming red hair, her beautiful smile, generous breasts, and shapely legs had first attracted him to her. But it was the woman inside that had kept him at her side for most of the night. He was surprised when she had accepted his invitation to go out. However, she had been the one who had suggested church at six o'clock on Sunday morning. At first, he had thought she was joking. She didn't know Louie didn't go to church. After he had looked in those large, green eyes, there was no way he could have refused her.

Other women liked Louie, but they never took him seriously. Louie didn't blame them. He was hardly marriage material. At times, he wished he could be like other men and have a steady home life and children. He had had his opportunities. Sally Rica had tried for almost two years to 'tie him down.' She would have made a good wife and mother. But not for Louie. He knew his place in this world and on this particular morning, it was in Elko with Wanda.

When he reached his black Model T Ford parked directly in front of the church, he found the half-filled pint of whiskey stashed under the front seat. He unscrewed the top with a flourish.

"To Wanda," he said in a toast. He then lifted the bottle to his lips and drank a few deep swallows to wipe out the stale taste of last night's beer. "Well, let's get the show on the road."

He wiped off his lips with the sleeve of his coat, replaced the bottle under the seat, and danced a jig to the front of his car. It was battered from minor crashes and encounters with ditches and was held together mostly by baling wire. Louie leaned down, grabbed the handle, and gave it a few good cranks. Nothing.

"Come on, Lizzie. We got to get to Elko," he whispered gently.

He kissed the palm of his hand and then gently caressed the hood. Bending down, he gave the handle another few turns. After a hint of waking up, the motor went back to sleep.

"Hey now. Don't do this to me," he said in a quiet voice.

He planted his legs firmly on the road, leaned down, and gave the crank a few quick, hard turns. This time there wasn't even a suggestion of life.

"Start already," he yelled. He threw in a few damns and hells as if they would help start the car. He cranked again, about ten quick turns. Nothing.

This time he swore even louder. Louie's father had mastered the practice of using the Lord's name in vain and Louie emulated his father perfectly. His curses echoed over the sleeping town.

He marched up to the front seat and again found the bottle. After several healthy gulps, he tossed the empty bottle on the front seat and stalked back to the front of the car. Looking up at the steeple clock, he could almost see the large hand move as it neared six o'clock.

He turned the crank steadily for about thirty seconds as fast as he possibly could. His hat flew off his head and rolled underneath the car. Finally, his hand slipped off the handle, banging against the fender. Louie grabbed his bleeding hand, wincing in pain.

The expletives flowed from his lips; his curses again echoed over the silent town. The volume of his voice rose as the crudity of his profanity increased. He swung his leg from as far back as he could and kicked the Model T so hard the car retreated about a foot.

"Damn. You would have to do this to me today!"

He was about to give it another solid boot when he felt a hand on the back of his shoulder.

"Damn it, leave me alone," he screamed. He turned around to see Father Doherty, stern pastor of St. Simon's.

"Louie, my son. Calm down. Your blasphemy is waking the whole town."

"My damn car won't start, Father."

"Louie. Louie. Blasphemy won't do any good. And if you keep on swearing like that, you'll never get to heaven."

"But Father. I don't want to go to heaven. I want to go to Elko!"

*   *   *

The statue of Jesus on the dashboard accompanied Louie to Wanda's house even as he exceeded the posted limits of forty miles per hour by at least ten miles. Father Doherty had miraculously agreed to allow Louie to use his car. He was adamantly opposed until Louie convinced him he had to pick up Wanda for church.

Louie reached under the seat for the bottle of whiskey that wasn't there. What kind of car was this anyway? It was immaculate. There was nothing on the floors, not even Father's footprints. The windows were so clean he could see out of them. The smell of incense permeated the air. It wouldn't have surprised him if Father Doherty used holy water in the radiator.

Louie was ten minutes late when he arrived at Wanda's house. She and her father were pacing impatiently in the front yard when Louie slid to a stop. Her father didn't seem any happier with him now than he had the previous night. Since Wanda was only nineteen and more than ten years younger than Louie, her father had kept a watchful eye on them the entire evening. Now it almost looked as if he had planned to attend church with them.

"You're late," he announced as he positioned himself between Wanda and the car. She peered around him at Louie with her heart-melting smile and blew a kiss toward Louie. And which Louie returned.

"Don't get smart with me kid," he huffed as he leaned in through the car window. "Wanda here says you're takin' her to church. That right?"

"That's right," Louie answered as he reached forward and pretended to reposition the statue of Jesus upon the dashboard. Wanda's father stared at the statue for a few seconds and then pulled back and opened the door for Wanda.

As the car pulled out of the driveway, Louie looked into the rear-view mirror at Wanda's father who was making sure nothing would happen to his daughter in his driveway. Louie glanced over toward Wanda. Her dress was made of the finest fabric and was tailored to accentuate each of her many fine features. Louie was wearing the same clothes he had on the night before.

"You look even more beautiful than last night," Louie said. "You didn't have to get so dressed up for me."

"I always dress up for church," Wanda answered which caused Louie's heart to sink. "But not as much as this."

"We better get a move on if we're going to make it," Louie stated. A huge smile covered his face. He shifted Father Doherty's car into third.

"We'll never get there in time," Wanda replied. "Besides, I really don't want to go now. God will forgive me if I don't go this one time. Won't He? What I really want to do is ride around and see my new town. I've been here two weeks and I've hardly been off the farm."

The next two hours Louie showed Wanda the sights. Actually, the sights took about five minutes; the rest of the time they were lost in their own world, completely oblivious to anything around them. They eventually found themselves stopped at the side of the road, Wanda's farmhouse looming across the field from them. Louie drew some courage from inside himself, not from the bottle as he usually did, and slid over the seat toward Wanda.

Wanda reciprocated and moved closer toward him. Their lips met in a kiss that had been suppressed since the previous night. Louie didn't want it to end. And then something made his hand move. Was it his arm? It had to be. His hand moved stealthily up Wanda's skirt. That's when Wanda's hand moved. Right across Louie's face.

"That's it! Take me home!" Wanda screamed, pulling her skirt down.

"What?" Louie asked.

"You heard me. Take me straight home!"

Louie started the car and slammed it into first gear. With a shower of gravel behind them, they sped off down the road. A mischievous smile appeared replacing the bewildered look on Louie's face. He turned the steering wheel sharply to the right. The car lunged off the road and disappeared into the ditch. Louie and Wanda watched as weeds completely engulfed the car. Suddenly the car arched upwards, and the bright blue sky appeared in the windshield. With a slam, the car landed in the freshly plowed field and continued diagonally over the rutted furrows towards Wanda's house. The car rocked from side to side as both Louie and Wanda bounced up and down in their seats, banging their heads on the roof of the car. Even Jesus himself jumped off the dashboard and hid under the seat. Rabbits and gophers scurried out of the way as the car hopped across the field. A huge furrow decided not to move and tore off the right front fender.

Louie looked over to Wanda who was screaming, not from fear but with joy. Her laughter filled the car by the time they came to a stop in Wanda's barnyard, the car's radiator boiling over and two of its tires flat. There they were greeted by Wanda's father. After a few choice words, he ushered his hysterical daughter toward the house. Louie followed them to the farmyard where he came face to face with Father Doherty.

"I brought your car out for you," he said, pointing to Louie's car. "I found it starts better if you turn on the ignition."

"Yeah, I guess that would help," Louie answered sheepishly.

"And where is my car?" Father Doherty asked.

Louie reluctantly ushered Father Doherty to his car. At first, all he could do was stare at it, eyes wide open in astonishment.

He finally could contain himself no longer.

"Louie! My car! My God in heaven! What have you done to my car? Holy Jesus! Lord have mercy!"

"Now, now father," Louie said calmly. "Keep that up and you'll never get to heaven!"

THE END

DANCEHALL DAZE

Everything had been decided for me. Like where I was born. And to which family. While Annette Funicello and Frankie Avalon frolicked on the beaches of Southern California carrying surfboards, I slaved on farm fields in Minnesota spreading manure.

But not this night. It was a Saturday night in the summer. I had a few dollars in my pocket. And maybe, just maybe, I might finally meet a girl.

As I drove my dad's gray 1950 Ford down Main Street, I glanced toward the Star Bar and Grill. The door swung open. Out stepped a former classmate, Phil, a girl hanging on each arm like fuzzy dice dangling from the mirror of a 1957 Chevy. He was tall and scrawny with hips no bigger around than his waist, a waist barely wide enough to hold up his new blue jeans. His blond hair was slicked back with Brylcreem or Vitalis. His attempt at facial hair was reminiscent of a sparse lawn suffering from the burning sun of August. He wasn't the best-looking boy in the class. But he was a town kid, a rich town kid.

I slowed, rolled my window down, and called out to them. They looked at me, or through me, as I continued down Main Street.

When I neared Hank's Drive-In, a small diner about the size of a railroad car, I noticed the town's attempt at a gang congregated at a picnic table. Bear, Pickle, JD, and Prune, in their twenties, and thirty-five-year-old Smokey Joe puffed on cigarettes as they tried to look cool and dangerous. They wore jeans with the waist down on the hips and the bottoms rolled up revealing white socks and black shoes. They had white t-shirts with a pack of cigarettes, probably Camels or Marlboros, rolled into the top of their sleeves. JD waved to me as I passed, a one-finger hope no one notices kind of wave. Pickle grabbed a runty fourteen-year-old from the front of the line at Hank's and took his spot at the window.

I stopped in front of the Corner Bar across from Gehlen's Jewelers to let Mick and Andy, a Laurel and Hardy-like pair, jaywalk across to Ike's Bar. A horn blared behind me. I looked past the reflection of my acne-covered face at a red Ford Mustang behind me. The honking stopped once I moved. In front of the bakery, three high school boys in a black 1957 Ford were pulled next to the curb trying to talk three teenage girls into riding with them. One of the girls stood at the open car trying to coax the other two reluctant girls into the car.

At the end of Main Street, I turned around at the entrance to the cemetery, the grass worn down to dirt in front of the No U-turn sign. I pulled back onto Main Street and headed back into town behind Sam Sawyer on his red Farmall tractor. Sam usually 'dragged the Main' in his 1952 Chevy for hours each night. But a week ago he had lost his license after he was caught drunken driving one too many times. Now, much to the annoyance of the town cops, Sam and his tractor cruised Main Street about a hundred times each night.

When I again reached the Star, I saw Phil standing next to his fancy, new green Ford Thunderbird, the T-bird looking like a wounded duck with its hood up. The two girls, Penny and Sue, leaned against the fender. Phil spotted me and flagged me down. Sure, now I was good enough to notice. I pulled behind the T-Bird and rolled down my window. Phil slowly sauntered over to the car and leaned into the window.

"How's it going, Maynard?"

"Better than you, I guess. What's wrong with your car?"

"Someone stole my battery. Can you believe that?"

"No, I can't. Who would do something like that?" I answered. I wish I had thought of it.

"Say, we're going to the dance. How about if you give us a ride?"

"Sure, I guess," I said. I hadn't cleaned out the car before I left the farm. Dust from feed sacks still covered the back seat. All the farm smells were still ground into the upholstery. While Phil went back to get the girls, I reached back and tidied up the back seat the best I could. I found a cob of field corn and threw it into the glove compartment just as Phil opened the back door. Sue slid into the back seat, her skirt sliding up her thighs revealing more of her black mesh stockings. She was followed by Phil, who was then sandwiched in by Penny. Great. One of the girls could have at least sat in front with me. Now I was nothing more than a chauffeur.

I looked back at the three. "All comfortable back there?"

"You know, Phil," Penny said, completely ignoring me. "It's too bad they don't have phones you could carry around so you could just call your dad right from the middle of Main Street."

"Don't be stupid, Penny," Phil answered. "That will never happen. They have to be hooked to a wall with a cord."

"You'd need a cord a mile long," I added.

Phil, Sue, and Penny just stared up ahead at me like I was the village idiot.

"And everyone's phone cords would just get tangled up with everyone else's."

They continued to stare at me.

"I guess I'll just head to the dance, then," I said.

If I had been born a 'town kid', I would be the one sitting in the back seat between Penny and Sue. It just didn't seem fair. Actually, I wouldn't need two girls. Either Penny or Sue would be okay with me.

I passed Sam on his tractor. It could be worse, I thought. I could have been born Sam. It could be worse yet. I could have been born Penny or Sue, which would put me next to Phil. This was too much to think about.

"Don't you have a radio in this car?" Phil shouted.

"Yeah."

"Well, play it then, why don't you?"

I reached over and turned on the radio. The radio came on to KDHL and the sounds of the Six Fat Dutchman playing the polka, *In Heaven There Is No Beer*. Immediately, the three in the back seat broke out in laughter.

"You listen to that stuff!" Phil laughed. "That's what old people listen to."

"Yeah. Old farmers," Penny chimed in. "My uncle listens to that. He must be almost thirty!"

I fumbled with the radio dial.

"My dad listens to this station," I said. "For the farm reports and…"

The laughter from the back grew louder.

"Oh, never mind."

I found WDGY playing *The Wanderers*. That was better. Up ahead, the dance hall lights illuminated the early evening sky. Cars swarmed toward the lights like mosquitoes and bugs to the yard light on the farm. I couldn't wait to get there. I was sure Phil and the girls were as eager to be rid of me as I was of them.

"Will you need a ride back after the dance?"

"Naw. My brother Jack will give us a ride back."

Thank God.

I turned the corner past the ballpark and the Park Ballroom came into view. The red and blue neon sign shined brightly above the canopied entrance. The 'B' was burned out, converting it to an allroom. I found a spot about a block from the door. As soon as the car came to a stop, the doors opened, and Phil and the girls darted out. In seconds, they were gone. Without a word.

"Thanks for the ride, Maynard!" I said aloud to myself.

I got out of the car and moved toward the entrance. Just ahead of me were Jim and Nancy. They were so close together they were almost one person. They seemed completely unaware of anyone or anything around them, something that hadn't changed since they had first met as freshmen in high school. I couldn't imagine anyone feeling that way about me. I followed them through the line, purchasing my ticket from Mr. Peterna, my old high school English teacher, who worked at the dance hall as a summer job.

"Hello, Maynard. Still dangling those participles?"

"What? Maybe. I don't know. Yes. No." I don't know why he always made me nervous. Maybe because I never got dangling participles.

"Wearing short skirts, I saw all the girls," he said. "You better go in, then."

Inside, the music reached a deafening roar. Couples swung each other around the dance floor. The rock and roll band, 'The Four Drifters', dressed in yellow pants and black jackets looked like bumblebees. I wandered toward the concession stand. I noticed girls standing along the wall or congregating in groups near the dance floor. Would I ask one of them to dance? I had asked and been refused so often. Their most common response was, 'I don't feel like dancing'. Then why the hell did they come to a dance? Why did I keep asking?

I bought a Coca-Cola and stood at the corner of the dance floor watching Phil and Sue dance. I felt a tap on my shoulder. I turned to see Penny. Was she asking me to dance?

"Maynard. I forgot my purse in your car. Could we go get it?"

"Sure. I guess we better."

From behind Penny, another girl appeared. She had a beautiful smile. Was she smiling at me? Was she actually smiling at me? She was plain in comparison to Penny. But with her smile, she looked more beautiful.

"This is my cousin Jane."

The three of us walked to the car. Penny talked constantly. About Phil. Phil this and Phil that. Jane and I couldn't get a word in. We just smiled at each other. By the time, we got back to the dance floor, my mouth hurt from smiling so much. We met Phil near the bar where he had just purchased four bottles of Grain Belt Premium using his fake ID. Penny joined Phil and Sue and another guy I had never seen before.

The band started its next song. I wanted to ask Jane to dance but it was one I didn't know how to dance to.

"Do you want to dance?" she asked.

"Uh. No," I answered.

"Then what did you come here for?"

"I mean. I don't know how to dance this one."

She grabbed my hand.

"Come on. It's easy."

She led the way to the middle of the floor. Despite a few awkward moments at first, I felt more comfortable. By the end of the song, it looked like I almost knew what I was doing. The next song was rock and roll. That I could do. My cousin had taught me that at wedding dances. I realized that I was finally having fun while dancing. One song blended into the next. Time just flew by. Finally, a slow song started. She moved toward me and gracefully folded into my arms.

"I'm having a great time," she whispered into my ear, sending a shiver up and down my spine.

"Me too. How come I've never seen you here before?" I asked.

"I've seen you before."

That surprised me. Someone had noticed me.

"We just moved here a month ago," she continued.

We passed under a mirrored ball that threw different colored lights over us. So, this is what I've been missing.

I felt a tap on my shoulder. Someone was cutting in. How could that be? Not now.

"What's that old farmer doing here?" Phil asked.

I turned around to see my dad. He was dressed in overalls, boots, and a farmer's cap.

"Not now, Dad," I said.

"I need your help."

The band announced their break. Couples cleared the dance floor leaving my dad, Jane, and me standing under the mirrored ball.

"The cows got out."

"Damn. Okay. I'll be right home, Dad."

"I'll go with you," Jane said.

"Oh, yeah," my dad said. "You left for the dance before I could show you this."

He handed me the letter and walked off the floor.

I just stared at the envelope. There was no need to open it. I knew what it would say. Why now when I had just met Jane?

"What is it, Maynard?" Jane asked.

"Jane. It's from the draft board. I think I've been drafted."

Jane herded cows from the field into the pasture. She was still wearing her white dress from the dance. In the moonlight, she looked like an angel.

Of course, there is always that one cow that tries to get away. Jane ran over to block its path. When she stopped suddenly, she slipped and fell into a mud puddle. When she got up, I saw that her dress was covered in mud. She herded that last cow into the barnyard, and I closed the gate.

"You must have grown up on a farm. You're almost a pro at this," I said.

"Almost."

"Except for the part where you fell down," I said.

"Except for that. I grew up with six younger brothers and sisters. Same principle. But no. I'm a farm virgin. I mean, this is the first time I've ever been on a farm."

"You could have fooled me."

I grabbed a flashlight and we headed toward my dad who was fixing the hole in the fence.

Jane said, "I don't get it. Why would the cows try to get away?"

"You know the old saying. The grass is always greener on the other side."

"I know. But look. They've got everything they need right here. Food. Water. And they escape to what? A plowed field and a country road where they become targets for any passing car."

Up ahead, the lights from the pickup lit up the gap in the fence. The radio on the pickup was tuned to KDHL and old-time polka music. My father tightened the bottom strand of barbed wire. He had the middle and top wires to go. I looked over to Jane and stopped her.

"I don't get it. You just met me and here you are. Wandering around in the middle of the night. You probably ruined your dress. And look at your shoes."

"It's okay. I have other shoes and dresses. But this. This is sort of an adventure."

"An adventure! Try living it twenty-four hours a day. Every day."

"For me, it's an adventure."

"Then there are a lot more 'adventures' out here for you. Like milking. And cleaning manure out of gutters and…"

"Okay. Okay. Stop. The real question is. Did you open the envelope?"

"No. I've been kind of busy. Besides, I know what it says."

"You need to know. For sure."

"Strange," I said. "I just met you tonight. And, well, I never could talk to girls. And here we are. Talking like I've... You know. I've never talked to anyone like this."

"Quit stalling. Open it already."

I pulled the envelope out of my pocket and tore it open. I shined the light from the flashlight on the words 'Greetings from the President of the United States.'

"It says I have to report to Minneapolis in three weeks. For induction. Just three weeks."

"That's not much time," Jane said.

"No, not much."

"Why couldn't it have been Phil, instead?"

"He'll never be drafted. His dad is the head of the draft board."

"You could try to get out of it somehow"

"I couldn't do that. I figured if I was drafted, I'd go in."

"Are you crazy?"

"No. I was even thinking of enlisting like my dad did in WWII."

"You are crazy."

"It might be best if I did go to Vietnam. To help end this thing. It's just like on the farm. Sooner begun. Sooner done."

"Then maybe I should enlist, too," Jane said.

"Now who's crazy?"

"Three weeks," she said. "What are you going to do with *all* that time."

"I was thinking. Maybe we could spend some of it together. If you want to."

"You know," Jane said. "That's the best idea you've had tonight."

I took Jane in my arms, and she rested her head on my shoulder. There, under the full moon and a sky filled with stars, we danced to the Roman Rezac Orchestra playing the *Blue Skirt Waltz*.

THE END

ACKNOWLEGDEMENTS

A special thanks to my writers' group in Minnesota, The Writers' Rung, and to my writers' groups in Florida, the Fiction Writers' Group of Tarpon Springs and the Palm Harbor Writers' Group for their tremendous support and feedback

Cover photography by Curt Tilleraas

Made in the USA
Monee, IL
02 December 2021

83700622R00152